Franny Parker

Franny Parker

Hannah Roberts McKinnon

SCHOLASTIC INC.
New York Toronto London Auckland
Sydney Mexico City New Delhi Hong Kong

ISBN 978-0-545-24393-3

Published by Scholastic Inc., 557 Broadway, New York, NY 10012, by arrangement with Farrar, Straus and Giroux, Inc.

12 11 10 9 8 7 6 5 4 3 2 1 10 11 12 13 14 15/0

Printed in the U.S.A. 40

First Scholastic printing, January 2010

Designed by Jonathan Bartlett

For Grace, my reason for everything

Franny Parker

The Facts

When Grandma Rae Parker stole me away to the preacher on the morning of my kidnapped christening, she told him, "Bless this one just a mite bit more, if you will, dear reverend. She may be a Parker, but she's got her mother's look in the eye." For that fact I am proud, because what Grandma Rae didn't understand was that any trait shared with my mother was already blessing enough.

Daddy says Mama is part wolf. Mama's love has teeth. Like the wolf who carries her pups real gentle in her mouth, then curls her lips back to show a sharp mouthful when she feels the need to be protective. That's how Mama is with her pack. And that's what Grandma Rae never understood.

Now about the kidnapping, I don't remember any of it, being just a tiny baby at the time. I've got to rely on the story as Mama tells it, in a quiet moment before she tucks me in. Or as Daddy tells it at the dinner table, his eyes crinkling with laughter.

Grandma Rae, being who she is, thought she was doing a kind thing in sneaking my baby self to the preacher like that. Of course, Mama and Daddy didn't know. They thought I was safe asleep in my crib down the hall. They were in the kitchen making pancakes, with no intention of having me christened on that day or any other day, according to Mama, so I can imagine they were none too pleased. But Grandma Rae wouldn't hear of raising a baby without the Lord's official blessing, and said it was bad enough Daddy had gone and married Mama, who was what she called a free spirit. So that balmy summer morning she put on her Sunday best, and she took me off to church. All a secret, until Mama got a feeling she should put down her pancake and go check my crib. The mother wolf has instincts.

By the time they figured out where I was, I was christened. Of course that was a long time ago. It's what you'd call a family story, one that may not have started out too funny, but has sort of smoothed out its hard lines over the years, each voice that tells it wearing down the jagged edges like wind on a mountain. We can laugh when we tell it now; the story's gotten so it's not so sharp when we hold it. These days when we recall it Mama just shakes her head and laughs in a light way that ripples like water. "It was a gesture, Franny," she tells me. "Sometimes even the kindest ones get boxed up wrong and arrive on your front porch in pieces. You've just got to try to remember what it started out as, is all."

ooo

I finally understood what Mama meant the summer of my thirteenth year. That summer there were many good intentions that turned out just fine, and quite a few that turned out all wrong. Like the Fire Department's Fourth of July bonfire. The whole town gathered at the swimming hole, ready for a night of barbecue, toasted marshmallows, the works. But there would be no fire. Hours later, those sticks were just smolder and smoke. Kids cried, and the firemen held up their hands in apology. That was the picnic where we all ate our s'mores cold and hard. The firemen must've felt awful bad 'cause the next week they held a redo. And boy, was it! You could roast your marshmallow from fifty feet back. Finally they had to call in one of the trucks and hose down the barbecue. But no one complained. Everyone ate their charcoaled hot dogs in their soggy buns. We knew the firemen had tried their best. Mama was right about good intentions. This is the first thing you need to know.

The second thing is the importance of family. Our family is very close, and by that I mean that some of us are close in how much we like each other, and some of us are just close in geography. Grandma Rae says it makes no difference. "Franny," she says, "family is all you've got." On the walls of her buttercream parlor hang pictures of Daddy's Oklahoma roots. Deep roots, back to the first settlements in the Cimarron Valley. Grandma likes to refer to those pictures often, especially the ones where skinny-legged farm kids stand like poles, hands crossed stiffly in front of them. Very respectful, she tells us. Personally, I think those kids look miserable. But I like looking at my people.

Only a bike ride away from Grandma's is our farmhouse, with its crooked porch swing that's never empty for more than a minute, and Mama's flowers busting out of the shrubs that line our porch. Out of control, as Grandma Rae says. In the back, Daddy's vegetable garden rolls down our sloping yard to the river, and by August, when it's close to bursting, it unravels itself, leading a parade of tomato and pepper and squash right to the water's edge. In the fall, we keep an extra close eye on the pumpkin vines so we don't lose a good jack-o'-lantern down the river. It's happened before. Across the way is the red barn where my chestnut pony, Snort, lives, and by it the old silo leans toward the fields where Daddy likes to bird-watch, almost like it's pointing to our well-traveled route into the hills. My little brother, Ben, and I liked to lose ourselves in those fields, though it seemed a little harder to get lost each summer as I got older.

Finally, you need to know that summer is a state of mind. Picture the way it looks on a person: a sticky ice cream mustache, a late-afternoon hammock dream, a gauzy dress rolled loosely at the knee. Summer has a mood different than any other season, and it sort of infects people. Maybe it's the hazy afternoons that go on and on, or the too-sweet lemonade, or the full-bellied moons that hang extra low in the sky, but I've noticed that kids and grownups are under a bit of a spell come summer. It usually strikes around July, and you can always tell when it starts. People act just a little crazy: gardening in the hot sun, wading into a farmer's stream, declaring love beneath dark windows. Mama calls it summer fever. And that year the fever started on the same day a blue truck rolled into the neighbors' driveway, the first Friday of July, beyond our red barn.

Plans

"No turtles at the table!" Sidda shrieked.

"But he loves you! L-O-V-E loves you!" Ben giggled, dangling his pet turtle, George, over Sidda's plate.

"Mom, make him stop!"

I covered my ears before I even reached the kitchen.

"Well, look what the cat dragged in!" Daddy said by way of greeting me. He handed over the last piece of bacon with a wink.

"All right, everyone, what's the plan?" Mama asked. She pulled a pencil from the thick tangles of her curly hair.

"I'm off to the pool," Sidda announced, fussing over the pink skirt of her new bathing suit. Even though my sister was just a year older than me, she was a professional teenager.

"Well, I'm off to the bank," Daddy said, gathering up the morning newspaper. "After I stop by the river bend. I think that egret has an egg in her nest." His eyes flashed with excitement. Daddy was a loan officer at Morton Savings, but most people in town called him the Bird Man. He never left home without his binoculars.

Ben peered at his scrambled eggs suspiciously. "Is this egret?"

"Of course not," Mama replied with a smile. "It's dinosaur."

Ben's eyes widened. "Cool! T. rex for breakfast." And then he stood on his chair and abruptly launched into his day of friends and swimming lessons and peanut butter sandwiches and more friends, which basically boiled down to one word. Camp.

"Whew!" Mama laughed, pretending to wipe her forehead with exhaustion. "You are the busiest five-year-old in town!"

Ben nodded proudly. "It's a tough job," he said, reaching for another pancake.

Mama turned her smile on me. "How 'bout you, Franny?" she asked.

I shrugged. "Just taking care of the patients," I said.

Mama nodded her approval. In June I'd started a bit of a makeshift hospital for injured animals in our backyard barn. Just like Mama, I was a lifelong animal lover, and it seemed I had a special knack for crossing paths with broken-winged birds or orphaned mouse babies. It had turned into quite a project for the whole family, except for Sidda, of course.

"I have an idea," Ben whispered, reaching into his overalls pocket. "Babysit George and Martha." He placed a second turtle right on Sidda's plate.

"Eew!" she shrieked.

"You mean turtle-sit?" I asked.

"It'll only cost you fifty cents," Ben stated. He clapped his hands as George climbed slowly over Sidda's toast.

"Ben," Daddy said, "I believe *you're* supposed to pay the person who does the sitting."

Mama pulled Ben down by his overalls and smacked a big kiss on my head as she swept up his lunch box and the loose turtles in one hand.

Ben caught my arm in a sticky-milk grip. "Okay, okay. I'll only charge you twenty cents. Please, Franny?"

Sidda smirked. "She's got no plans. Other than her stinky critters."

"How would you know?" I asked, watching them stand from the table.

"I'm sure Franny has all kinds of excitement planned," Dad said, grabbing his car keys.

"Don't forget to feed them lunch," Ben told me, as he placed his turtles back in their bin. "You'll have to dig up worms. Big, fat ones."

Mama smiled sympathetically from the doorway. "I'm dropping Ben and Sidda off, then going shopping. No riding Snort until Daddy or I get home, right?"

I nodded glumly. The Parker Pony Rules of Safety. I'd heard them for years, and had yet to break one. Helmet, boots, grownup. Check, check, check.

"I believe these are for you," Sidda said as she dropped a plastic bin at my feet with a disgusted thud. I peered at the two turtles inside. They were carefully nestled on a bed of damp moss, rocks, and leaves placed around the plastic perimeter. Ben's true loves.

Dad was wrong, I thought. No exciting plans for me.

Until I heard the crunch of tires on gravel.

New Neighbors

I was ankle-deep in river mud, on worm patrol for Ben's turtles, when I heard it. Peering up over the riverbank, I caught sight of a faded blue Ford pickup truck veering left, where the driveway split to the neighbors' empty cabin. It had been empty over a year. Now, the truck rolled to a stop and the doors swung open on either side.

Woo, woo, woof! Jax, our yellow Lab, sprang off our porch and loped across the yard.

"Get back here, Jax!" I hollered, clambering out of the riverbed after him. He looked over his shoulder as if to say, *I know I'm a bad dog, but I just can't help it.* I chased him next door as a woman lowered the tailgate with a bang and began pulling boxes off the truck. Big boxes, like the kind that mean you plan to stay awhile.

"Lucas, come help," she called. In response Jax leaped up and licked her nose.

"Well, you're not Lucas," she said to him. She smiled at me, pushing at the long hair piled on her head, all wispy. Pretty. I smiled back.

"That's Jax," I said, reaching out to shake hands. It was then I realized I was still holding a worm. There it was, wriggling in my hand, right under her nose. Not knowing what else to do, I stuck the worm in my pocket and shrugged.

"Sorry about that. I'm Franny."

She laughed, and to my surprise she shook my wormy hand anyway.

"Did we interrupt your fishing?"

I looked at my dirty feet, feeling shy. "Oh, no. The worm's for my little brother."

The woman frowned.

"For his pet turtles," I explained.

"Ah, well, it looks like a good juicy one. I'm Lindy. And this here," she said, pointing to a boy climbing out of the cab, "is Lucas."

The first thing I noticed about Lucas Dunn was his eyes. They were gray-blue, like the stones Ben collects in the stream. They were cool and watery, and for just a moment they made me feel a little sad. His hair was light like Lindy's and he was tall. He looked down at my muddy toes and smiled. Suddenly I felt foolish standing there like a kid, saying nothing.

I sucked in my breath. "I'm Franny."

"Short for Frances?" Lucas asked.

"Francesca," I said, blushing. "It's my aunt's name."

"Nice." And he hopped onto the tailgate and began rummaging through boxes.

"Where are you from?" I asked Lindy.

"Oh, here and there," she said, taking down a box Lucas handed her.

I brought them lemonade while they unpacked, stacking the boxes on the dusty front porch of the cabin. They didn't have a lot, but what they did have was interesting. There was a heavy potting wheel, which took a lot of careful maneuvering to unload, that Lindy said I could try. And a small square kiln with a dented lid. And several boxes of clay she opened to show me. Red like the desert.

"I'm a potter," she explained, showing me her fingernails, dry and red like the clay.

"My mother's an artist," I told her. "Her hands are a different color every day."

Besides the pottery supplies, there was a giant box of books, barely stuck together with tape. Novels spilled out of the top, like they were leaping off the truck.

"My boy sure likes to read," Lindy said.

"Me, too," I told her, watching Lucas out of the corner of my eye.

In no time Lindy was pulling the last box off the truck. "Thanks for the lemonade, Franny. Come by for a spin on the potting wheel." And she disappeared into the cabin. Lucas followed, tossing a book in the air.

"Francesca, catch." And then he, too, disappeared into the little cabin. I looked down at the worn cover in my hand. *The Yearling*.

ooo

"Yay!" Ben shouted, when I announced we had new neighbors that evening before dinner. "Maybe there's a boy like me. Maybe he likes turtles!"

"Let's hope not," Sidda said, thunking down a dinner plate by my new book. "Move your junk, Franny, so I can set the table."

"Now, Sid," Mama warned. She set the leftover squash soup on the stove and turned her attention to unpacking the shopping bags strewn across the kitchen floor.

"There is a boy," I told Sidda, whisking *The Yearling* away. "About our age."

This sparked Sidda's attention, and now she was suddenly Miss Manners. "Well let's have them over! We are neighbors, after all." She finished with the plates and started on the silverware, pausing to admire her reflection in a giant soupspoon.

"So, you've met them?" Daddy asked, joining us in the kitchen.

"Yeah, Franny, how *do* you know?" Sidda asked, narrowing her eyes.

"It's just two of them, Lucas and Lindy." I turned to Sidda. "Lucas is the one who gave me the book." Her eyes widened.

"Good. There's a boy and he likes turtles." Ben nodded.

"We don't know that, Ben!" Sidda snapped.

"Well, it'll be good to have a new neighbor," Mama said. "Did they say where they came from?"

I shrugged. For all her talking, it was the one thing Lindy Dunn hadn't said.

Dad took over the groceries, and Mama carried a bag of new paints over to her easel in the family room, dumping them into her art bin.

Ben reached for a blue one. "Wow, *aquamarine*! I bet the turtles would love to be *aquamarine*!" he declared.

Sidda scoffed. "You are not painting those disgusting turtles!"

"But they're *painted* turtles!" He waved the tube at her.

"That's their name, Ben. Just a stupid name. It does not mean they are supposed to be *painted* aquamarine!" Sidda argued. Her hands were on her hips now.

I poked Ben, trying not to giggle. He was a master at stirring Sidda up.

"Mom," she complained, "tell him he cannot paint the turtles aquamarine."

Mama was unpacking canvases now. "Ben," she warned, but I could see the grin through her wavy hair.

"Okay, okay," he groaned, grabbing a tube of red. "Then how about *magenta*?"

Saddle Up

Early Monday morning, I was in the barn grooming Snort when a freckled face popped over the stall door.

"What page are you on?" Pearl Jones's wild red hair stood on end and Snort reared back in fright.

"Easy, boy," I said. "It's just Pearl." Pearl was my best and oldest friend, but her wild hair and sudden appearances never failed to startle the pony, or the family, for that matter.

The barn was the only place to escape the heat, and I'd spent the morning tucked in a corner of Snort's dark stall with *The Yearling*. Snort didn't mind.

"Want to ride?" I asked.

Pearl's eyes narrowed and she stared at the book resting on the stall door. "You didn't answer the question."

"Oh, Pearl, not again," I said with a sigh.

The summer reading frenzy had begun last month. Poor Pearl. Her mother had a hand in this, I knew. The Aubree Library began its annual summer reading contest the day school let out, and Mrs. Jones's eye was always on the lookout for a prize: in this case, $100 and a tall gold trophy for the kid who read the most books. Pearl, for being such a shy and reasonable girl, had the misfortune of a not-so-shy and rather unreasonable mother.

Pearl was the oldest child in a family of six kids, which meant she had the dubious distinction of being the first representative of the Jones family in every endeavor the public might witness. No accomplishment or event occurred without Pearl's mother pushing her toward every opportunity for glory. During Girl Scout cookie sales, Mrs. Jones bought and ate every box that Pearl couldn't sell just to increase their tally. She gained at least twenty pounds. At soccer games, Mrs. Jones was known to stick out her foot when a girl on the opposing team ran into the sidelines. And at horse shows, Mrs. Jones would swat a pony playfully on the rear end, causing it to buck and launch the poor rider clinging to its back.

Despite her mother's foul play, poor Pearl still hadn't come in first place in anything. So this year her mother had aimed her powers at the reading contest as their big chance. Every moment was a reading moment, according to Mrs. Jones. Pearl even had to read in line for the ice cream truck at the town pool. Mrs. Jones most likely wouldn't notice if Pearl was drowning, but Pearl had better not lay out her beach towel without at least two books on it.

"So?" Pearl asked, swiping at a red curl hanging in her eyes.

"Page thirty," I said, giving up. "How's Nancy Drew?"

Pearl frowned, sinking onto a bale of hay. "Boring, that's how."

"Let's go for a ride," I said, dusting off my saddle.

I went to the tack room for Snort's saddle. The day Mama had given the saddle to me was the day I got Snort, four years ago, on my eighth birthday. I'd been tearing through the presents looking for a brush, a hoof pick, any sign of a pony. As the pile of presents got smaller and smaller, I'd tried to put on a brave face. A diary from Sidda, a sweater from Grandma Rae, a macramé necklace from Ben. When all the boxes were open, I sat in the pile of wrapping paper and thanked everyone, trying hard not to let the tears pushing at my eyelids escape. And then Mama took my hand, pulled me out to the porch, and led me to the swing where it sat. A saddle with a big red bow. *Her* childhood saddle. The same tired old saddle I'd climbed onto in our attic for years. And now it was mine. With my very own pony to wear it.

Of course there were stories that came with this saddle, and Mama had told me each one over the years. Every nick or scratch in the leather was a memory. "This," Mama said proudly, "is from the time Shadow bolted through the woods on a narrow trail. I think a bobcat spooked him. And this"—she pointed to a dent—"is from the time Shadow slipped on Turtle Creek, and we skidded down the bank into the river rocks." I'd never met Shadow, but I could see him in my head like a red flame, him and eight-year-old Mama racing through the forest, setting the branches ablaze. Her best stories involved near danger and horses, and so it was real hard for me to follow her Parker Pony Rules of Safety after listening to them. I always felt like I was missing out on something.

We brushed Snort quickly, concentrating on his sleek brown back.

"Is that him?" Pearl asked, gazing out the barn door.

"Who?"

Across the way, Lucas Dunn stood on a ladder, his back to us and a paintbrush in his hand. One side of the cabin was coated in fresh white. He worked quickly, the muscles of his back flickering with each stroke.

"What's he like?" Pearl breathed, a flush of red creeping up her cheeks. I touched my own.

"I don't know," I lied. But I did know. In just the three days since Lucas Dunn had arrived, I knew a lot. I knew that Lucas liked to listen to the peepers at night, that he stayed up well after his mom had gone to sleep, and wandered by the low riverbed. I knew that he liked to peel the skin off an apple with his Swiss Army knife before sinking his teeth into the firm flesh. And that he preferred walking barefoot in the grass. Ever since he had arrived, it seemed Lucas Dunn loomed outside my window, in my backyard, as plain as the yellow moon in the sky. Wherever I turned was evidence of his being.

He waved, looking suddenly over his shoulder. "Hey, Francesca!"

Pearl stiffened beside me, a goofy smile plastered on her face. "Wow." She sighed.

"Come on," I said, dragging her away. "Snort's waiting."

Animal Hospital

Mama says the ways of our family put a bee in Grandma Rae's bonnet. Especially our way with animals. The beginning of July marked Aubree Library's annual tag sale, a weeklong event where townspeople donated all their old stuff to the cause. Sidda claimed she had no interest, but Ben and I loved to pore over the tables of discarded treasures. Last year I'd discovered a book on Norwegian ponies, and Ben found himself a one-eyed stuffed monkey. So on Tuesday morning we headed off to the sale, our saved allowances in hand, and bought ourselves a yellow cat. The cat wasn't actually for sale, but it was the most exciting thing we could find amid the droopy boxes of attic clutter. Ben spotted it first, crouched behind a box of old books, probably waiting for a mouse. It was a fine cat, a bit raggedy about the ears. You could tell all it needed was a good supper.

"We'll take him!" Ben told the two old librarians, Miss Thorn and Mrs. Tibble.

"Oh, honey, I don't believe that cat is for sale," Miss Thorn said politely. "He's just a stray."

But Mrs. Tibble recognized a hungry buyer when she saw one, and she could tell Ben wasn't about to leave without the cat.

"Fifty cents!" she barked. "He's half price."

"Sold!" yelled Ben, who thought we'd gotten ourselves quite a bargain.

Grandma Rae and Mama were shelling beans on the porch as we marched home with that cat in our arms. Ben was proud as ever, and he would've skipped the whole way except the cat didn't seem too pleased about the skipping part. We had to share the carrying as it was; four arms help to distribute the scratches. When we finally reached the porch stairs, we held out that tabby like we'd won the state lotto.

Mama looked up first. "And how long does that tabby plan to visit?" I could tell she wasn't pleased, but Mama never turns away a stray.

As soon as Grandma Rae's eyes lit on the cat, she leaped up and the beans went flying. "What in heaven's name are you doing carting that filthy animal around town?" She spun around and faced Mama. "Honestly, Celia, you let those kids drag home all kinds of garbage."

Ben and I hung our heads, but we exchanged a sideways peek. We knew better than to leave when the good stuff was just getting started. Mama wouldn't let us down.

"Now, Rae, I don't see the harm. The children will be responsible for the cat, and I can't see what kind of lesson it would be to turn away *one in need*." At that, Grandma Rae plunked herself back down, mouth in a twist. Accepting and assisting those *in need* was the theme of the preacher's sermons that summer, and if Grandma Rae was going to command our attention to those weekly sermons, then Mama was going to put the preacher's words to good use. To us, she said, "That cat can stay in the barn. You may get it some dinner, and then wash up for your own." Yes sir, Mama was a lifelong animal lover, worse than all the rest of us. I pictured her as a wide-eyed little girl, a mouse in her dress pocket and a dog at her heel. I ached to be just like her.

As we headed past the garden, Ben started in on cat names. "How about Jasper? Or Marmaduke? Oh no, what if it's a girl? I know! Cynthia!" Even with my back turned, I could feel Grandma Rae's disapproval burning a hole right there on the porch.

"And so it continues," she complained loudly.

Grandma Rae was referring to what had started a few weeks earlier. It was turning out to be the summer of those in need. It seemed that once your eyes recognized one, the needy were all around, even in unexpected places. That spring had been the driest on record in over fifty years, and by the end of May, Blue Jay's apple orchards had barely a blossom. By June it was worse. With no real rain all spring, the farmlands were crackled brown, and the wheat fields were in poor shape for harvest. The Wakeman family had such a bad crop that Faye Wakeman began working mornings at Harland's Market to make ends meet. Then there was a brushfire that almost wiped out the garden club's roses behind the church. These were terrible things, of course, but there wasn't a whole lot I felt I could do about them. Until one late June afternoon, the last day of school, much to Ben's horror, Daddy had found a painted turtle with a cracked shell on the side of the road. And so began our animal hospital.

"Who could do this?" Ben shouted, hands clenched in angry little fists.

"She's an old beauty," Dad agreed, tracing her wide shell admiringly.

We carried her to the barn, where we fixed her up good with yellow industrial tape. She looked just like a crooked highway lane, the lines running right down her bumpy shell.

"We'll call her Speed Bump," Ben decided.

It was then I got my idea for the animal hospital. And since that June day I'd been working real hard helping the needy, just as Grandma said. It wasn't exactly her way, but it was my own. And that was all that mattered.

While Grandma Rae busied herself arranging help for the Wakemans and carrying her own well water to the town rose gardens, she offered only a stiff look of disapproval to the old turtle, who we set up in a quiet corner of our barn, our first official patient.

Word spread quickly in town. By the middle of June, the mailman had brought us a box of baby birds, five barn swallows, who'd fallen out of a nest. The day after that Faye Wakeman had called from Harland's Market with news.

"Franny, I've got you some more patients," Faye said.

Ben and I hopped on our bikes and pedaled the two miles into town under the scorching sun, holding our noses past the Piels' pig farm, then coasting gratefully into the shade of the town green. We just about collapsed with relief once inside the air-conditioning at Harland's. Faye handed us cold pops and slid a cigar box out from under her cash register.

"Darrel would laugh me out of the house if he knew I'd delivered these little guys to you, but I just didn't have the heart to leave them," she told us.

Inside the box, five pink bodies stirred. Their dark ears were pressed tightly against their heads like flower petals, their smooth tails wrapped protectively around one another like a little nest.

"Ooh, mouses," Ben whispered.

"Found them under a hay bale. Must've scared their mama off. Can you help 'em?" Faye asked.

I stared at the mouse cluster. They had an alien look about them. "Mama will know what to do," I told Faye.

"You're a good girl, Franny Parker." Faye handed me a five-dollar bill. "Take this for your trouble."

Mama looked hard at us when we got home. "This animal hospital of yours is a huge responsibility," she said.

"I can do it!" I assured her.

She peeked inside the box and gasped. Mama's practical side was no match for such a sight. "Mother Nature," she whispered, examining a clawed paw in her hand. "She sure knows her stuff." I had to agree. From the whiskered noses to the round bellies, I had never seen anything so perfectly formed on such a small scale. Just waiting to fill up their space in the world. "All right then, call the vet. You'll need puppy formula and eyedroppers."

I showed Mama the five dollars Faye had donated to our cause.

"Start saving," she said, handing me a coffee can.

And I had been. All since June, right into the first week of July, I saved every cent and put it in the can I called "the Animal Funds."

The night we brought the yellow cat home, I traipsed down the hill to the barn with buckets full of formula and fruits and vegetables for all my patients, including a can of tuna fish. The air was cool and light, a faint breeze stirring the trees. And something else: music. Just like the breeze, it floated across the air from next door. The cabin windows glowed warmly, and inside I could see Lindy bent over the stove, swaying a little. The table was set, and there in one of the chairs was Lucas. His blond hair fell forward as he hunched over a book, a wide smile on his face. As I opened the barn door, I wondered what he'd read that made him smile like that. I turned on the lights and saw the many faces staring back at me, the glowing eyes of the animal patients nestled in my barn. I wondered if Lucas would like the sound of an old cat's raspy purr. I wondered if he, too, would grow all warm and fuzzy feeling the tiny heartbeat of a little bird pumping in the safe palm of his hand.

Dinner Guests

"There is a boy!" Sidda whispered gleefully, as though she had conjured him up herself. It was the middle of the week, and she was filling her best friend Marilee in on the latest, Marilee having been away visiting her cousins. "He moved in last Friday. He's tall and blond, and I must say he seems very nice," she said assuredly into the phone.

"How do you know?" I asked from the doorway of the room we shared. Sidda cupped the phone secretively and spun around.

"It is not polite to listen in on grownup conversations, Franny."

"I didn't know you had any," I muttered, collapsing on my bed with *The Yearling*. I'd been working my way happily through a series of horse books that Mama had gotten me for my summer reading, but I found myself setting them aside in favor of *The Yearling*. Lucas was right. So far, there was everything to like about the main character, Jody. He had himself a little orphaned fawn named Flag. And a disapproving mother who reeked of Grandma Rae. Sometimes I felt like I was reading about myself.

"His name is Lucas Dunn," Sidda purred into the phone. I stared hard at Sidda, leaning back in her chair, his name rolling comfortably out of her mouth. Up until then the discovery of Lucas Dunn had been largely my own. Now it seemed she, too, had been watching. When I couldn't stand to listen anymore, I headed for the kitchen.

At the counter, Dad was seasoning drumsticks and dipping thighs in batter. "Feel like fried chicken?"

"What's all the fuss?" I glanced at the neatly set table, the two extra chairs.

"Neighbors are coming."

"The Dunns?" I asked, panic spreading through my body.

"Should be here any minute," Dad answered.

I rushed back upstairs to my room and smoothed my hair in Sidda's mirror. Sidda was off the phone, sprawled across her bed, turning the pages of a fashion magazine. I smeared a dab of her cherry gloss on my lips, feeling a little bit like a thief. A smooth-haired, shiny-lipped thief.

"They're here," Ben shouted from the hall.

"Who's here?" Sidda asked, stretching lazily.

"Oh, just the new neighbor," I said with a casual shrug. "You know, the tall blond one you think is so nice."

"What? Now?" She hit her closet like a bullet.

"Somebody's trying to make herself *beauty-ful*!" Ben giggled in the doorway.

"Out, both of you!" Sidda screeched.

Ben and I raced downstairs to the door, where Lindy was handing Mama a big bunch of sunflowers.

"What a great farmhouse!" she said, stepping inside and looking up at the old beams.

"It's a work in progress," Daddy said. "The progress being a lot slower than the work."

Lindy nodded. "Old houses are a handful, but I think they've got good souls."

"Me, too," Mama said with a grin. I could tell she liked Lindy already.

Sidda sashayed into the room then, a swirl of pink skirt. She extended her hand dramatically to both Lindy and Lucas as Mama introduced them. I cringed. Didn't Sidda realize how ridiculous she looked?

"Why don't you kids give Lucas a tour?" Dad suggested, pulling my ponytail.

"Ben and I have to feed the patients," I said.

"Patients?" Lucas asked.

"Just some pathetic animals Franny has," Sidda explained, rolling her eyes. "I'll show you around." She looped her arm in his.

"Actually, I think I'll tag along with Franny, if that's okay," Lucas said, politely unraveling himself from Sidda's grip. Clearly this was not okay with Sidda, but Lucas didn't seem to notice.

"Follow me," I said, trying to hide my smile. "You can feed the turtles."

"How do you feel about worms?" Ben asked, as he handed Lucas a bucket on the porch.

The barn was cool and dark, the animals quiet. I lifted each mouse up from the soft heating pad in the shoe box. They squirmed and peeped, mouths open for the eyedropper.

"Where'd you learn all this?" Lucas asked in amazement.

"Some my parents taught me, some I taught myself," I said, feeling suddenly proud.

Ben changed the water in the turtle cage while I showed Lucas one of the baby birds.

"Wow, she's a beauty," he whispered behind me. I could feel his breath on the back of my neck, warm and steady. The little bird chirped as I scooped her up.

"A barn swallow," he added, leaning in closer. A thrill sprang to my chest.

"Yeah, how did you know?" I asked him.

"We had whole nests of them back in our barn," Lucas said.

"You had a barn, too?"

"A big old tobacco barn. It was my grandpa's, back in Georgia."

I watched him settle the hay gently around the bird as he

described the barn, delicately replacing each piece of straw until Daddy called us in for supper.

The table was beautiful. Mama had laid out some of her mother's creamy white linens, and the beeswax candles glowed above the small feast Dad had made.

"Lucas helped feed the patients!" Ben shouted, as we took our places around the table.

"Quiet down," Mama murmured, tucking a napkin under his chin.

"What'd you think of our little hospital?" Dad asked, passing his famous potato salad.

"It's great," Lucas answered shyly. "Franny's real good with the animals." I blushed, and Sidda scowled at me across the table.

"Lucas is a bird expert, too, Daddy!" Ben announced. "He had barn swallows at his old barn, too."

Dad looked up. "Really? You must've had the violet-green swallows in New Mexico. Never seen one myself."

Lucas looked puzzled. "Violet-green?"

"Yes, that's the variety of swallow that lives in the more western regions," Dad explained. "They winter in New Mexico."

"I thought you were from Georgia," I said.

"Georgia? You mean New Mexico," Sidda said, gazing at Lucas.

Lucas coughed and popped a potato in his mouth, looking suddenly uncomfortable.

"No, no, no," Ben corrected Sidda. "Lucas is from Georgia. He told me so!"

"No, no, yourself, Ben. Lindy was just telling us about their old house in New Mexico," Sidda insisted.

Everyone looked up in confusion, first at Lindy, then at Lucas, who both seemed to be just as lost as the rest of us.

Finally, Lindy cleared her throat. "Well, we moved here from New Mexico. But we also lived in Georgia, uh, some time ago," she tried to explain, looking at us hopefully.

"You certainly are well traveled," Mama said.

"I'd love to see a violet-green," Daddy said dreamily, still stuck on the birds. "Tell me, are they the same size as our barn swallows?"

"Um, I'm not sure." Lucas looked helplessly at Lindy.

"Mr. Parker is a bird-watcher," she told him, eyebrows raised pointedly. "He knows about birds, from *all over*."

Lucas shifted uncomfortably in his seat. Something wasn't right. "I don't really remember, sir." He shrugged apologetically.

"Well, you sure know your local birds," Dad said, his eyes crinkling with admiration. But the Dunns grew oddly quiet.

"What other critters did you have in New Mexico?" Mama asked.

"Um . . . I don't really remember," Lucas stammered.

"Crocodiles?" Ben asked.

"Don't be ridiculous!" Sidda said.

"Prairie dogs?" Ben continued.

"Something like that," Lucas said. He looked to Lindy again.

"You must remember some," Ben pressed.

"Ben!" Mama scolded.

Lucas looked like a cornered animal. It made my stomach flutter.

"Well, this sure is good chicken!" Lindy said, changing the subject suddenly. "I'd love the recipe."

"Want to share?" Ben asked, waving his half-eaten drumstick at Lindy. Everyone laughed, and comfort filled the room again. I looked around the table. Daddy sipped his wine. Sidda poked at her plate, still sulking. But Mama was looking at Lucas, her expression soft and worried. Just like I felt.

The Library Contest

"As you know, the first prize is a trophy and one hundred dollars," Miss Thorn reminded us the following morning, smiling down at the kids crowded around her feet in the children's section of our library. It was a few weeks into our summer reading contest, and Miss Thorn felt a little reminder of the prize money might prove motivating.

"Not to be squandered on junk!" Mrs. Tibble added, yanking a book cart to a sudden halt behind Miss Thorn's chair, like a dark shadow. She leaned ominously over the cart. "Personally, I find it's bad enough you kids think you ought to be paid for reading. A good book should be reward enough!" She slapped the top of the cart for extra emphasis.

Miss Thorn cleared her throat delicately and said, "I'm sure the winner will use the money wisely."

Ben raised his hand. "What about worms?" he asked. I elbowed him.

"What about them, dear?" Miss Thorn asked.

"Speed Bump eats worms. Could I buy a hundred dollars' worth of worms?"

"Who eats worms?" Miss Thorn looked puzzled.

Mrs. Tibble threw up her hands in disgust. "Oh, for Pete's sake!" She turned to go, shoving her book cart with a giant heave, the back wheel wobbling crookedly in protest.

Soon a frantic sea of hands was waving and everyone was inquiring how the money could and couldn't be spent. Ice cream? Skateboards? An iguana? It was exhausting. As far as I could tell, none of the kids with the silly questions were likely winners in the first place.

"What book are you on?" Pearl asked, as we hopped down the library steps. I was so tired from waking up every few hours to feed the mice that I wasn't in the mood to have this talk.

"My third," I lied. I was really on my seventh.

"Oh," Pearl said and sighed. She fingered her Nancy Drew book. It was the second in the series.

"Hurry, girls, hurry," Mrs. Jones ordered. She was parked in front of the library, squished into the driver's seat of her red convertible, her pearl necklaces spilling over the steering wheel. Mrs. Jones was large. Her car was not. I shimmied into the tiny backseat, pressed tightly against Pearl's baby sister, Mable, who was already sandwiched behind her mother in a car seat.

"Woof!" Mable barked, waving a soggy Cheerio at me.

"You mean *hello*," corrected Mrs. Jones. Not even the baby was allowed to enjoy baby talk.

I sank into the seat, pulling a Cheerio off my shorts.

"Hurry, Pearl, I'm burning up!" Mrs. Jones wailed again, fanning herself with her long sparkly nails. Her red hair was drawn back severely, and her pasty skin glowed sharply against the red car wrapped around her. Mrs. Jones looked like a peeled, hard-boiled egg stuck behind the wheel.

The car was hardly practical for a family of eight, and so two or three kids were always being left at home. Although Mrs. Jones said she liked the wind in her red hair, I suspect she didn't mind a few missing kids from time to time either.

"So give me the update! Who's in the lead?" she asked as we spun away from the curb.

"Julie Mills," Pearl shouted above the roaring engine.

"Again? She won last year!" her mother shrieked. In front of me, Pearl sank a little in her seat.

"So how many? Don't tell me. Three, four?"

Pearl sank lower. "Twelve."

"Twelve?" Mrs. Jones almost swerved off the road. She tore up Main Street, past Harland's Market and the feed store. Pedestrians fled the crosswalks as we blazed by the post office, the Methodist church, and Tweedy's Bakery. We passed Grafton Tractor Supply and the firehouse at warp speed, then swerved left at the hospital, heading out of town to the farms. Moments later, we roared down my dirt road like a red rocket, halting in a cloud of dust in front of my house.

"Franny, what about you?" Mrs. Jones glared at me, her forehead wrinkling in the rearview mirror.

"Um, three books," I lied again.

Her forehead smoothed out, and she said, "Well, Pearl, that is just one more than you. Franny's no threat. But twelve? That Mills girl is lying. I'm calling her mother!"

I climbed out of the car and shrugged apologetically at Pearl, who looked like she might break free and run with me into my house. But there was no chance.

"Buckle your seat belt, Pearl. We've got books to burn through!" her mother yelled.

The Sewing Bee

"That's a fine stitch," Grandma Rae said, peering approvingly over Sidda's shoulder.

Sidda beamed, tilting her part of the quilt up for everyone to admire. I didn't see what was so great about it.

"And you?" Grandma eyed me. I showed her what I'd been working on. "Oh dear. Better give it here."

I sighed and surrendered my square. Sewing just wasn't my thing. The Busy Bees, as Grandma Rae called them, came most Fridays. Daddy called them the Busy Bodies. They'd been at it for years, making quilts for new babies, donating shawls to the cancer wing at the hospital, wrapping each family member in their work. But it was more than just the sewing. Those ladies could spin a story. Every Friday afternoon I got to know a lot of people, most of whom I'd never met. There were second cousins from back east, rich uncles in California, even a runaway bride with a broken heart. Each of Grandma's friends had family, and family makes for good stories. When those ladies filled the room, our creaky old farmhouse felt solid, as if the party of chatty women inside made it stand up straighter on its ancient foundation. There was something about that group of women gathered around our kitchen table that made the walls nearly hum.

So far it was Sidda who showed the most promise in the family. I don't know who was more pleased by this useless bit of news, Sidda or Grandma, but both seemed to get great pleasure from informing me and Mama of their sewing superiority. Despite the fact only one girl in our family showed any talent or interest, somehow the Busy Bees had set up hive at our place. Mama, being a free spirit, didn't mind a bit. She dragged her easel in from the living room and painted right alongside them at the table. And I liked seeing Izzy, Dotty, Faye, and Grandma tottering up our porch steps with bags full of fabric and mouths full of stories.

The latest project was a patchwork quilt with a giant oak tree growing out of the center and into the sky, leaves and birds sprinkling the branches. So far it was just an ugly brown hulk of a trunk. The tree had a lot of growing to do.

"Today's hotter than a flapjack," Izzy said, pushing her giant straw hat back on her head. Grandma's friend Izzy was as wild as her hats. She was known to decorate the wide brims with just about anything, from green bananas to lightbulbs.

When Ben was a baby, just the sight of her crazy hats used to make him cry. But he got over that. Today's hat was covered in tiny plastic dinosaurs that swung around each time she turned her head.

"How are the fields?" Grandma Rae asked Faye, ignoring Izzy's dinosaurs.

"Not so good," said Faye. "We lost most of the wheat back in June. Cotton's due for harvest in August, but it doesn't look much better. We may have to apply for government aid this year."

"It's turning out to be a bad drought," Mama said, planting a glass of lemonade in front of me. "I saw the state trucks over at Larsons' farm last week. They were inspecting the south fields. Apparently they've already declared their sorghum crop a total loss."

I'd seen the state trucks around town, too. Red pickups with Oklahoma government stickers on their sides. They only came out during disasters: floods, drought, dust storms. The sight of those red trucks meant farmers were asking for state money.

"Isn't there something we can do?" I asked, thinking of the low river in our yard, the yellowed fields behind Snort's barn.

Faye shook her head sadly. "Not unless you can bring my two hundred acres back to life."

"We've done stranger things," Izzy replied, swatting at a T. rex that swung dangerously close to her left eye.

"Don't remind us," Dotty Knox said.

"What kinds of things?" I asked.

"Oh, you know, prayed at church, made casseroles, helped irrigate fields. It's always something each season."

"That's not all we do," Dotty whispered.

"What are you talking about?" I asked them.

Mama swirled some red onto her palette and adjusted her canvas. It was a new one, a portrait of a woman in a red coat. "These girls have all kinds of powers, Franny. They can conjure up the rain."

A hush fell over the group.

"You're just joking," Sidda said. "No one can do that."

"Oh no?" Izzy's eyebrows went up and down, up and down.

The ladies set down their quilting, and spoke a rhyme together, their voices soft and light in the afternoon heat.

Dance in a field to the crickets' tune,
a full-moon sky in the afternoon.

Sidda and I looked at each other, then at the ladies, who resumed their stitching quietly.

"That's just silly," Sidda said.

No one disagreed.

"If it is true, why didn't you bring the rain for Faye's crops? Or Blue Jay's apple orchards?" Sidda said. She had a point. I looked around the table to see how they'd handle that logic.

"The time has to be right," Dotty whispered.

Outside, there was the sudden crunch of gravel in the driveway, and the spell was broken. The blue truck rounded the corner to the little cabin.

"New neighbor?" Izzy asked.

"Lindy Dunn," Mama told them. "She moved in last week. Has a boy Sidda's age."

Izzy winked at Sidda, who fluttered her eyelashes.

"What's the husband like?" asked Dotty.

"Doesn't seem to be one," Mama said with a shrug.

"No husband?" Dotty pressed.

"Not our business," said Grandma Rae, but she, too, waited for Mama to answer.

"Husband or not, I'll tell you what she has got. Talent. She set up a pottery studio in the garden shed," Mama said.

Faye nodded in agreement. "She brought some of it down to Harland's just yesterday. Bowls and vases, all sorts of colors. Real pretty."

I'd been in that potting shed myself. Tucked behind the back of the house like a little secret, it was a small garden shed that Lindy had done up like a cottage. She'd hung plaid curtains in the windows, planted flowers in the boxes, and squeezed her worktables neatly into each corner. She often worked late into the night, and I always knew when she was done because the wind chimes would ring through our open window as she slid the heavy door closed. I liked the thought of the shed windows glowing in the darkness, and Lindy working her hands over the clay inside it. I pictured her at her wheel, humming softly, while the night unfolded outside. In no time at all, she'd become as much a part of the night as the river gurgling behind our house and the peepers beneath our window.

"We should meet her, girls. How 'bout next week?" Izzy asked.

Mama shrugged. "I'm not sure if she sews, but I'm happy to invite her."

"Next Friday," Izzy said, yanking the T. rex from her brim. "She'll come."

Bug Cakes

"Ouch!" Ben yelped as Sidda swatted him with the wooden spoon.

"Hands off, it's for my guest!" Sidda said. She was elbow deep in a bowl of pancake mix.

I couldn't tell which looked worse, our kitchen or Sidda. Batter splashed the countertops and floor. I wondered what the fuss was about. After all, Marilee had eaten breakfast with us hundreds of Saturday mornings.

I watched as Sidda turned her attention to the refrigerator. It was a doozy, crowded with all sorts of animal concoctions for the patients. You had to be real careful what you reached for when you stuck your hand in there. More than once Daddy had accidentally poured the mouse formula in his coffee.

Crickets were the most gourmet item on the patients' menu, loved by Speed Bump and the birds alike. So I stored a big old bowlful in the fridge. Right next to the bowl filled with blueberries. And that's just what Sidda was reaching for. Gabbing away on the phone to her friend Amanda, she stuck her arm in and grabbed the bowl of crickets.

Before we knew it, she'd dumped those crickets right into the pancake mix. She couldn't figure out why it was so lumpy, so she just kept stirring. Ben and I covered our mouths in horrified delight. Sidda just kept on talking; stirring and talking, flipping and talking. Soon, she had herself a whole stack of cricket pancakes and was buttering them up good when there was a knock on the kitchen door.

"Come in, Marilee!" Ben shouted. But it wasn't Marilee joining us for breakfast this Saturday. Instead, Lucas Dunn poked his head in the back door and smiled.

"I got a call about some pancakes," he said.

"You're here!" Sidda shrieked, swiping at the pancake mix on her cheek and smoothing her hair with her sticky fingers.

What was Sidda up to? I looked over at Mama's fine blue china, the table set for two in the adjacent dining room, and it all walloped me in the head.

Ben and I exchanged looks. This called for a change in plans. It was one thing to watch Sidda eat cricket pancakes, but Lucas? It hardly seemed fair.

"Can I help with anything?" Lucas asked, starting toward the counter.

"Oh no, no." Sidda laughed nervously, directing him to the dining room table. "You sit yourself down and I'll be right out. It's almost ready!"

Sidda hurtled back into the kitchen with a pitcher. "Make yourself useful, Franny," she hissed. "Pour us some juice." She dusted herself off and picked up her pancake platter with a flourish.

"Sure," I whispered, watching as she scooped up the pancake platter. "But perhaps you should try your special pancakes before you serve them. You know, to be sure they're perfect."

Sidda stared at the pancake platter before her. "Yes, of course. They do have to be perfect." Then she looked at Ben and me. "But don't you dare sneak a bite for yourselves!"

This was too much for Ben, who giggled himself right off his stool. "We wouldn't dream of it!" he yelped.

Ben and I were about dying as we watched Sidda pour the syrup over the platter and pick up a fork. She cut herself a tiny bite and dipped it in the syrup. It took forever. By then Mama had joined us in the kitchen, and Ben and I tried to look as innocent as possible.

"Sidda, how lovely to make breakfast for Lucas," Mama said.

"Blueberry pancakes," Sidda said, her fork poised in midair. "Fresh from the garden."

Mama opened the refrigerator. "Did you forget the blueberries?" she asked, holding up the bowl just as Sidda popped the forkful into her mouth.

It didn't take long. Sidda looked at the empty cricket bowl, at the empty fork in her hand, and then at me. I would bet ten dollars that you could've heard the scream clear into town. I didn't mind. Lucas ate cold cereal on the porch with me and Ben, while Sidda recovered in her room under a cold washcloth.

Poor Sidda. Never again would she even look at a pancake.

Mailboxes

It still hadn't rained. Not in May, June, or even now, going on the third week of July. Each day dust clouds fluttered around our feet, settling between our toes, covering our skin in gray layers. The drought dragged on. "The worst in over thirty years," people whispered at the post office, on the library steps, and in line at Harland's. I felt like I was wilting.

"Better keep the water buckets full," Dad told Ben and me. "It's gonna be another scorcher." He set the Monday paper on the table, gulped his coffee, and kissed us all goodbye. "Try to stay cool. I'll see you after work."

"Well, don't count on me to fill buckets," Sidda informed us. "I'm meeting Marilee at the pool. We have to get there early to get the good lounge chairs." Sidda had been in a foul mood all weekend, on account of the crickets. Now she wanted even less to do with Ben and me, or the animals.

"Drop your brother off at camp?" Mama asked, clearing the dishes.

"But it doesn't start until nine!" Sidda argued.

"Perfect!" cheered Ben. "I'll have time for a swim."

"But, Mom . . ." Sidda complained, her blue eyes wide with offense.

"Or," Mama continued, "you could always help out here."

Sidda huffed away from the table, snatching her beach bag from the closet. "He's got five minutes," she said, slamming the screen door. “And don’t even think about bringing those turtles!” she yelled toward his room.

After I’d filled Snort’s water trough and watered all the animal patients, I found Mama seated at her art desk in the family room. She rifled through her paintbrushes, a small can of red paint in one hand.

“Working on your portrait?” I asked, glancing at the woman on the easel.

“Nope, working on the mailbox today. Grandma Rae suggested a new coat of paint. Says it’s so faded she can’t read our name anymore.”

I rolled my eyes. “We wouldn’t want Grandma Rae to go to the wrong house.”

Mama smiled. “Come help, so we’ll be sure she doesn’t.”

I sat on a patch of dry grass at the end of our driveway, watching Mama swirl the red letters of our name, “Parker,” the “P” large and cheerfully potbellied. As bossy as Grandma Rae was, I had to admit it looked real nice when Mama finished.

“What about Lindy’s?” I asked, looking over at the Dunns’ plain black box.

“Mmm,” Mama said, examining the box. “It does look a bit dark and serious.” In no time she’d spelled out “DUNN” in large block letters, adding a little flower at the end.

“Much more handsome,” she said with a laugh.

“Dashing!” I agreed.

“Excuse me.” It was Lindy, hurrying out to the road. “What are you doing?”

"Oh, hi," Mama said. "We were sprucing up our mailbox. Figured we'd do yours, too. You don't mind, do you?"

Lindy forced a smile, but it was an uncomfortable one.

"Oh, you don't need to bother," she said, stuffing her hands awkwardly in her back pockets. I looked at Mama.

"It's no bother," Mama said. We stared at the new box, still wet with fresh paint. "I'm sorry," Mama added suddenly. "I should've asked you first."

Lindy shook her head. "No, no, it's real nice. It is. I just hadn't planned on putting our name on it. Out here for everyone to see." She looked around nervously.

"I can change it if you like," Mama said, holding up her brush.

Lindy sighed, then shook her head. "No, no, it's okay. I guess I'm being silly. I should be thanking you."

"You sure?" Mama asked. Now she looked as uncomfortable as Lindy.

"I'm sure," Lindy said with a nod. "Now, how about some iced tea? You girls must be hot."

Mama accepted, clearly relieved, and they headed off to the cabin.

"You coming, Franny?" they called.

"Right behind you," I answered. But instead I studied Lindy's mailbox. The letters were straight and sharp, pleasing to look at. What didn't she like about it?

Plentiful Seasons

Afternoons were the worst. There just wasn't any escape from the heat. The animals drank up the water as fast as we could drain it from the barn pump. I put my lips to the nozzle, gratefully swallowing the cold water that came from the deep dark ground. Jax wiggled between my knees, his pink tongue lapping at the faucet. Suddenly he turned, and a deep *woof* worked its way up from his throat. I turned, too.

"Is the doctor in?" Lucas Dunn leaned against the door as if he'd been doing it all summer. Jax wagged right up to him, slobbering away at his open hands.

"Hey!" Ben waved. "Where you been all week?"

I'd been wondering the same thing. It was Wednesday afternoon, and we hadn't had a visit from Lucas since the pancake incident over the weekend.

"Been working," Lucas said. "Got me a job down at Harland's Market."

So that's where he was.

"Well, come see Speed Bump," Ben said. "She's almost fixed."

Lucas followed him into the stall. "Nice work, guys." He ran his hand gently over the tape, tracing the rough surface of her shell, his fingers following the patterns and grooves. "Do you ever wonder if turtle shells are anything like fingerprints? You know, how no two are ever alike?"

"Like snowflakes!" Ben shouted, growing excited.

"Yeah. They tell a story," Lucas said.

"What about rings on a tree?" I wondered out loud. Lucas looked over the stall door at me, and our eyes locked.

"What about them?" he asked.

"Well, rings on a tree tell a story," I explained. "They tell you about its seasons, if they've been plentiful or not. The rings show how much water the tree's had, how much nourishment, that sort of thing."

Lucas gazed past me for a minute, nodding thoughtfully at the hills beyond the barn. I began to feel uncomfortable, like maybe I'd said something silly, but he smiled at me.

"Plentiful seasons," he finally said. "I like that."

Lucas stayed through the afternoon, scrubbing buckets and cleaning out cages. He answered every one of the hundred questions Ben threw at him, from what armadillos eat for breakfast to where stars go when they fall. I wasn't so sure about his answers, but he never lost patience, or told Ben to stop. I realized I liked him best for some of the things he didn't do.

When the work was done, Ben went inside to cool off and Lucas and I plopped ourselves on the edge of a hay bale, sinking gratefully against the wall. Jax settled at our feet, resting his chin quietly on his paws. The scent of dry grass rose into the air around us. It was sweet and dusty, like the day.

"Oklahoma always this hot?" he asked.

I'd forgotten he was still a newcomer.

"Hotter than a flapjack," I said, borrowing Izzy's line. "We sure need rain." We sat like that awhile, Lucas chewing on a piece of hay, me counting the wild beats of my heart, hoping Sidda wouldn't spy us from the window, or Mama call for dinner just yet.

"What do your rings say?" he asked, reaching suddenly for my hand.

"What?" It startled me when he wrapped his fingers around my wrist, turning my palm up so he could see it.

"The lines on your hand. What do they say about your seasons?"

I thought about the old elm tree outside my window, how it creaked on windy nights all year long. About Speed Bump's rough shell, marked by turtle seasons; laying eggs, having babies, hibernating. And the rings of my life: Mama and Daddy, Ben, Sidda, and Grandma Rae, the farm, this dusty little town. All of it rising inside me over the years, so familiar, yet as new and strange to Lucas as he was to me.

Lucas's fingers were cool against the heat of my hand, and he moved them gently over my palm as he studied it. I tilted my head and took him in. His hair, the same color as the hay we sat on, his skin freckled and brown. He smelled like summer, like grass and sun and earth.

"What does it say?" I whispered.

"Well, for starters it says you've had plentiful seasons. Good family. Great dog." He nudged Jax with his toe. "And you're at home in the outdoors. You're no scaredy-cat."

"I'm not?" This surprised me, my heart pounding harder in my chest, as if to say, "Oh, if you only knew the truth!"

"No scaredy-cat I know would run a hospital for wild animals!" he said, motioning to the cages and stalls.

I smiled proudly and withdrew my hand reluctantly from his. "What about yours?" I asked, feeling brave.

He hesitated, but let me take his hand. "So?" He raised his eyebrows playfully.

"Hmm, it says you also like animals. And the outdoors. That you come from lots of places. And a nice family."

At this he pulled his hand back.

"What?" I'd said something wrong.

"Nothing," he muttered, his hand twisting in his lap. He turned to me. His face was so close to mine that our noses almost touched. "You're wrong about something."

"What part?"

"The family part. My family, well, it's different from yours."

"But your mom is great," I said.

He nodded. "Yeah, I know. It's just that my seasons haven't been so plentiful."

"You mean your dad?"

He looked away. "I don't have a dad," he said firmly. "He's dead."

Neither of us said anything for a long time. We just sat in the doorway of the barn, letting the heat press lazily against us. The barn felt both peaceful and sad, the animals in their stalls with no mothers, Lucas sitting on the hay with no father. He sighed before covering my hand with his.

"I'm just glad to know you, Franny." He looked at me hard, his eyes like the river outside the barn, watery and hopeful.

"Dinner!" Mama yelled from the porch. I jumped then, reclaiming my hand, stuffing it nervously in my pocket. Lucas hopped up, dusting himself off, and we hurried out of the barn. We walked together partway up the yard, to where the path split just beyond the garden, returning us both home. Him to his quiet little cabin, me to the busy farmhouse, the coiled rings of my plentiful seasons turning noisily inside me.

Invitation

The kitchen table was a mess of purple tissue paper and sparkly stationery when I headed in for dinner. I'd brought in the box of baby mice to show Mama, but from the looks of Sidda's project there wasn't a sparkle-free space to put them.

"Marilee turns fourteen next Saturday," Sidda announced. "And I've been elected her official party planner." She licked an envelope dramatically and sealed it with a kiss.

"Birthday cake!" Ben whooped, punching the air with his fist.

"You," Sidda told him, pausing to lick another envelope, "are not invited."

"Aww, Mom," Ben wailed.

I picked up a purple invitation.

"No rodent fingers on the cards, please," Sidda said, snapping the card out of my hand.

I stuck out my tongue.

"Sidda, perhaps you can move your work off the table so Franny and Ben can set it," Mama suggested, putting salad fixings on the counter. "How're the patients?" she asked me, pointing at the mouse box.

I set it on the counter and opened the lid so she could peek. The five babies stirred in their sleep, their little pink paws stretching. The littlest guy in the bunch yawned.

Mama beamed at me. "Wow, their fur coats have come in, Franny. Well done!" She was right, the mice looked great. But one was smaller than the rest. Ben called him Runty.

"I'm worried about Runty," I told her.

Mama nodded. "I know, honey. Mice are hard. He just needs a little extra attention."

Runty may have been the smallest, but he had become my favorite. I picked him up and settled him in the front pocket of my shirt. I could feel his tiny mouse warmth as he curled up to sleep.

"Hey, Mom," Sidda interrupted. "What's the Dunns' address?"

"Number four, I think."

"Why do you want it?" I asked, turning to look at her.

"Because we're inviting him to the party," Sidda said, inspecting her list and checking off Lucas's name with a flourish.

"But you barely know him!" I said.

Sidda dismissed this. "We'll be in the same class at school."

"Oh, I think it's a nice idea," Mama said. "Introduce him to some new people."

"Besides," Sidda said, "just because he likes your animals doesn't mean he's your friend. He's only being polite."

"Now, Sidda," Mama scolded, pointing a cucumber at her.

I was not prepared for the lump in my throat that came with Sidda's words. Suddenly I wanted to grab her invitations and tear them up. Instead, I turned away, pretending to busy myself with the mice. Sidda was wrong. Lucas was my friend.

After dinner, Mama found me at the kitchen stove. The mouse formula was just warming, and I stirred it lazily around the pan as Runty slept on in my pocket.

Mama sat down and studied me carefully. "You look tired," she said, pulling me gently onto her lap. It was something she did often with Ben, something I was embarrassed to admit I still longed for myself. I folded into her arms and closed my eyes. "Why don't you let Daddy and me do the late shift tonight?"

"But you said it was my job."

"I know, but everyone needs a rest now and then."

I thought about that, about how tired Mama herself looked some mornings, rushing around the house, her hands always full with breakfast plates or backpacks or bills. When was the last time I'd offered to help her?

"You don't mind?" I asked, getting up to take the formula off the stove.

"I like those furry critters as much as you do," she said.

"Maybe one night off would be good. I'll do it tomorrow," I promised her.

"I know you will. Go tuck them in, then get yourself to bed."

I grabbed the formula bottles and was halfway out the door when Sidda caught me.

"Pop these in the mailbox for me, will you?" she asked, her hands full of the party invitations.

I nodded and stuffed them under my arm.

"And don't spill any rodent food on them!"

At the mailbox I sorted through the stack of purple envelopes, holding each one up to the faded light from the porch so I could read the addresses. Lucas's was almost on the bottom. It looked like the others. I held it a long time before I lifted the red flag of the mailbox and stuffed the envelopes inside. All except one. I tucked Lucas's safely in my back pocket. I didn't plan to keep it. Not really. I needed more time to think about it. It wasn't just a party, after all. Once Lucas started hanging around with Sidda and the others, would he still be my friend?

After all, Lucas's mailbox was right there next to my own. I could just pop it in when I was ready. The other invitations would take at least a day or two to get to everyone. And I'd be saving the mailman a delivery.

With that decided, I slapped our mailbox shut. It was then that I noticed the Dunns'. Their box was black. Plain black. The letters of their name were washed clean away, Mama's red handiwork just a faint smear on its side.

The New Member

Lindy was a real hit with the Busy Bees that Friday, just like Mama and I knew she would be. She arrived with a loaf of lemon bread tucked under her arm and planted herself smack in the middle of the old women, like she herself was one of the Bees. She surveyed the quilted scene before her.

"What a magnificent tree!" she said.

Grandma Rae offered her a tiny brown square, a beginner one like mine. Lindy stitched the shapeless cotton into a graceful tree branch, and the tree took life before our eyes.

"My," said Grandma, sliding her glasses down her nose to admire the work. "Looks like you need another."

I noticed she reached for a tricky leaf pattern this time.

"Thank you all for inviting me," Lindy said. "We've only been here a couple weeks, and it's nice to feel a part of things already." Lindy glanced at the ladies.

"Oh, be careful 'bout thanking us too soon. You don't exactly know what you got yourself into!" Izzy exclaimed with a hoot.

"Speak for yourself," said Grandma Rae, patting the Bible that I knew was in her sewing bag. "This is an upstanding group," she proudly informed Lindy.

"I believe it," Lindy said, smiling.

"So how's our library?" Izzy asked. "There must be an awful lot of news down there!"

Lindy had started working part-time at the Aubree Library. After work she'd drag home an armload of books for Lucas.

"Oh, we have all kinds of news," Lindy said.

The Bees jerked to attention. "Such as?" they asked at once.

"Well," Lindy answered, "we get newspapers from three

counties, not to mention the Internet. You should stop by. I'd be happy to help you surf the Web if you haven't already."

The ladies wagged their heads.

"No, no, these bodies are too old to surf anything," Izzy said. "Besides, current events are not what I meant. I'm referring to the *town* news you must be exposed to there."

The ladies nodded in unison.

Lindy looked confused.

"Izzy means gossip." There, Mama said it.

"Oh, Celia, we do not gossip," Grandma Rae corrected. "Gossip burns the ears. We *share*."

"Ah, yes." Lindy nodded. She studied the group carefully and leaned forward. "Well, I may have heard a little something about the mayor's wife."

No sooner had Lindy opened her mouth than did every head bow faithfully in her direction, the quilt set aside for a "breather." Never mind what Grandma Rae said. Those ladies' ears were on fire! Mama winked at me from her easel.

"You certainly seem to have settled right in," Dotty said after Lindy finished, fanning herself with a napkin. The ladies were slumped in their chairs, plumb wore out from all their *sharing*.

"Your pots are quite the talk in town," Faye added. "Harland's can hardly keep them on the shelves."

Lindy smiled.

"I don't suppose you've attended Sunday service yet?" Grandma Rae asked, raising one eyebrow. We held our breath.

"Not yet, but I met the pastor at the farmers' market last weekend. Helped me pick out some peaches."

Grandma nodded in approval, casting a quick look at Mama. Like I said, Lindy was a real hit. Which is why we were so surprised by what Izzy said next.

"So where is your husband?" Izzy asked. Just like that. There we were having a grand time, and *boom*, a deathly quiet hit the room like a comet.

"Izzy!" Mama chided. Lindy looked at her hands. I saw the edges of dried clay around her thumbnails.

"It's okay," she said, sitting up straighter and facing the women. "I'm afraid I don't have one."

My thoughts ran back to what Lucas had said in the barn about his father. But Lindy didn't share any more. The ladies busied themselves with their leaves and branches, all except Izzy, who fixed Lindy with a gentle look.

Mama, sensing the need for an intermission, set down her brushes and palette. "Lemonade, anyone?" she asked. I followed her to the kitchen, where we worked the lemons back and forth over the wooden counter, squeezing the juices up to the surface. Mama sliced each one expertly, her long fingers moving over the yellow fruit, pressing each one to the juicer.

"Take these to the chickens," she said, passing me the peels.

Outside, I tossed the lemon over the chicken wire, watching as the hens squawked and scratched around the scraps. I headed up the hill and around to the back door by the kitchen. It was there I heard Izzy's voice join Mama's inside. They spoke quietly, so I knew they were having a private talk. I waited outside, trying to tell my ears not to listen, but I couldn't help it.

"Honestly, Iz, why'd you have to ask her that?" Mama scolded.

"Well, weren't you wondering the same thing?" Izzy asked.

"Of course, but it's not our place. Lindy's new."

"She didn't seem to mind," Izzy protested.

"She's just being a good sport," Mama said.

"Well, she's used to it."

"What do you mean?"

"A river of sadness, that one," Izzy said with a sigh.

"Don't be silly," Mama replied. "Lindy's the most cheerful woman I know."

"I'm not kidding. I've seen sadness myself, and I can recognize a woman who's seen the same." Izzy's voice was solemn.

I peered through the back window. Mama and Izzy were at the counter, the ladies chatting loudly at the dining room table behind them. I strained to hear Mama's words.

"Come on, Iz. She's got a great kid, she's settled in nicely. Her pottery is a hit."

Izzy shook her head. "Details, details, details. Look in her eyes sometime. There's a story there she's not telling," Izzy insisted.

Izzy took the lemonade to the ladies. I pressed myself against the house, breathing quietly against the wooden heat. The back door opened, and Mama walked right past me, a strange look on her face. She crossed her arms and stared hard at the little cabin next door.

Ice Cream

"So what book are you on?" Pearl wheezed, her skinny legs pedaling fiercely.

"My fifth," I shouted back, rounding the corner of the town green onto Main Street. I'd almost run out of formula for the patients over the weekend, so I was relieved to be on my way to the vet's office that Monday. For two miles Pearl had raced to keep up on her faded pink kiddie bike, its worn tires spinning twice as fast as those on my ten-speed. I glanced back sympathetically at the freckles glowing on her red cheeks.

"Mother says I can get a new bike if I win the library contest," Pearl had confided earlier. I don't know which made me feel sorrier, the fact that her mother was forcing her to ride a kiddie bike until she won or her belief that she actually could win.

I pulled up outside Harland's. "Ice cream break?" I offered, gently patting my shirt pocket. I'd taken to carrying Runty around in my pocket, letting him snooze in its dark warmth. He seemed to like it, popping his head out for a peek every now and then. I'd almost forgotten he was in there that morning until we were halfway into town.

"Okay," Pearl puffed, rolling to a shaky stop beside me. "Better hide that mouse." Pearl liked the animal hospital just fine, as long as she didn't have to touch any of the patients. Especially the mice.

We headed into the cool air of Harland's dairy section, and I peered into my Animal Funds can. I felt guilty spending the funds on ice cream. But Pearl had agreed to come along for vet supplies, so I figured I'd chalk it up to employee wages. Besides, the can was good and full at the moment. I'd long ago spent Faye Wakeman's first five-dollar donation, but there'd been plenty since from all the people who sent me new patients. Izzy herself had plunked a twenty-dollar bill in the can when Grandma Rae wasn't looking last Friday.

"Hey," Pearl said, handing me a Creamsicle. "Is that Lucas?" She pointed across the store to one of the cash registers. It was.

Suddenly I felt foolish with a mouse in my pocket and a melting ice cream in hand. "Let's go," I said.

"But I didn't pick out my ice cream yet." She stood in the middle of the aisle, hands on her hips. Honestly, sometimes Pearl was just like a mule.

"Take mine," I said, glancing quickly at the checkout aisle. I shoved the Creamsicle in her hand. "I'll meet you outside."

"Oh-oh," Pearl said, inspecting the redness creeping across my cheeks. "You like him."

"I do not!" I hissed. Pearl did not know what she was talking about.

I saw Mr. Harland approach Lucas's register and point to his watch. "Lunch break!" he said.

"Hurry," I told Pearl. I watched as Lucas pulled his Harland's Market apron over his head and tossed it over his shoulder. He closed his checkout lane and headed toward our aisle.

"Pearl!" I pleaded.

She looked me up and down for what felt like a long time. "All right. Let's go." She grabbed the ice cream from my hand and tossed it back in the freezer. Just as Pearl sometimes surprised me by reading my secrets, she also surprised me with these kindnesses. Small but crucial kindnesses. We hurried up the aisle, ducking our heads, but were stopped by a hideous scream.

"Rat!" a woman howled. "There's a rat in the dairy section!"

Instinctively, I felt my shirt pocket. Empty. We both spun around at once, to a scene that unfolded in slow motion. A large gray-haired woman was waving her purse with one hand and covering her eyes with the other as Jeremy Jenkins, one of the stock boys, ran around her in circles swiping at the floor.

"Stop!" I yelled. "He's not a rat!"

But they didn't seem to hear. Instead, the woman went on yelling and waving, until she got herself so worked up she collapsed on a crate of butter. Jeremy kept chasing the gray blur on the floor as it zigged and zagged up the dairy aisle, shoppers stumbling out of their path and milk jugs toppling to the floor. Finally Jeremy fell to his knees and smacked his hand over the floor. My stomach lurched.

"Don't hurt him!" I hollered, racing up behind him. Slowly he lifted one finger of his cupped hand. A whiskered nose poked out.

"Wait till Mr. Harland sees this!" Jeremy puffed.

"Please don't," I begged, lifting his fingers one by one to extract my mouse. "His name's Runty."

Jeremy shook his dark hair, hands on his knees. "We set traps in the back for these things."

I scooped Runty up and examined him quickly. He was fine. I looked back at the gray-haired woman, now wiping butter off her giant rear end. "So sorry, ma'am. I really am." She made no reply.

But someone else did.

"What's going on here?"

I whirled around to face Lucas.

"We're just leaving," Pearl said, grabbing my elbow.

"With their rat!" Jeremy blurted out.

"Rat?" Lucas raised his eyebrows.

"Mouse!" Pearl said. "Orphan mouse!"

Lucas looked around at the tipped boxes, the woman still trying to clean the butter from her skirt. He tried to hide his smile. "Well, you'd better scram fast," he said. "Before Harland comes."

"We have to tell him," Jeremy said, motioning to the mess. "I'm not cleaning all this up!"

Lucas turned to him. "Shall we also tell him about the *free* candy bars you eat in the back?" he asked, handing him a broom.

Jeremy looked away.

"Go on, Franny. Take your orphan home."

I flashed Lucas my biggest smile, and we took off. We were almost at the door when we crashed into Mr. Harland himself. He was not pleased.

"This is not a racetrack. You'll trample my customers!" Mr. Harland crossed his arms.

I nodded fiercely, covering my shirt pocket. I glanced over my shoulder, remembering the smashed boxes we'd just left. Pearl's cheeks burned crimson.

"We're very sorry, sir. There's something we should tell you—"

"Oh, here you are, sir." Suddenly Lucas appeared behind us. "Mr. Harland, these girls need your *expert* opinion."

Mr. Harland's eyes twinkled. "Oh?" Mr. Harland was a man of strong opinions, though it was not every day they were referred to as expert. He straightened his expert back, uncrossed his expert arms. "Why yes, yes, of course! What may I assist you with?"

Lucas nudged me and winked.

"Um, broccoli," I blurted. "We need your opinion on broccoli."

Mr. Harland nodded. And very gently, so you almost wouldn't notice, Lucas placed his arm on Mr. Harland's, guiding him slowly toward the produce section, one step at a time.

"And how are you preparing it?" Mr. Harland asked, wringing his mustache.

"Preparing it?" I wondered.

Mr. Harland looked impatient. "How are you cooking your broccoli?"

"We're making a pie!" Pearl shouted.

Mr. Harland cringed. "Broccoli pie?"

I closed my eyes.

"My mother's recipe," Pearl mumbled.

"I see." Mr. Harland thought this over, his brow furrowed

in concentration. Indeed, this was a job for an expert. "I can't say I've ever made broccoli pie . . ."

"Then what about banana?" Pearl asked, pointing to the display before us. Far away from the mess in the dairy aisle.

Well done! I thought, as we headed to the bananas.

Mr. Harland brightened. "We have wonderful bananas. Bright yellow, fresh-off-the-truck bananas!" He smiled widely, pleased with himself. By now we were in the colorful safety of the fruit section, standing before a giant case of yellow bananas. "Behold!" Mr. Harland pointed.

I glanced around. Lucas had long since disappeared. Surely the mess was gone by now.

"A fine fruit for a pie. Banana nut. Banana cream. Everyone loves bananas!" Mr. Harland was practically singing.

"Maybe we'll think it over," I said, inching back toward the door.

But Mr. Harland wouldn't hear of it. "Nonsense!" he cried. "Let's go, bananas!"

ooo

"You still owe me an ice cream," Pearl muttered as we pedaled away, our bike baskets loaded with bananas. I felt the soft ball in my pocket and breathed relief. The afternoon opened up around us, making me feel brave.

"Hey, Pearl, ever heard of a rain dance?" I asked.

"That's just crazy talk," she said.

As we turned onto my road I was about to correct Pearl, to tell her what the Busy Bees had said. But I was startled by the roar of an engine coming from the Dunns'. I stopped my bike where the driveways forked. Lindy would love the rain dance; I'd tell both her and Pearl about it.

But when I pedaled up, I saw it wasn't Lindy's truck I'd heard. There, in front of the cabin, a black car idled in a cloud of smoke. It was an old car, with a dented fender and broken taillight. I stopped my bike. A pale-faced man stared back at me from the driver's seat.

"This your house?" he asked in a gravelly voice. I flinched. Before I could answer, the man revved the engine and sped away, dust riding on the heat behind him like a dark veil.

The Black Car

It took me a day to get up the courage to face Lucas. Late the next afternoon I found him kneeling in his yard rubbing Jax's belly.

"Come get your ferocious dog," he teased.

"He bothering you?"

"Nah, he's a great dog." Lucas was right. "I wish we had one, but Mom says we move around too much."

"Well, you can borrow Jax anytime you like." I looked at Lucas, at the tan lines around his arms that peeked from under his T-shirt. "You're not moving away, are you?"

Lucas shrugged. "Not yet. Mom thinks the school here

sounds good. The neighbors aren't so bad either," he added with a grin.

I grinned back.

"So, how's the orphan?" he asked.

"Sorry about yesterday," I said. "You really saved us."

"No apology needed," Lucas said. "Most exciting lunch break I've had yet."

I blushed.

"What's Flag up to these days?" he asked.

"He's up to no good. Steals food from the garden, makes Jody's mother pretty mad. But he loves Jody so much, you can tell." I stopped, aware that I was blabbering away like a fool, but Lucas didn't seem to mind.

"Flag's pretty neat," he agreed.

"Jody, too. Can you imagine having your own baby deer?"

Lucas frowned. "But does Flag really belong?"

"What do you mean?"

"Just 'cause he's cute and follows Jody around like a dog, well, it's not the same. He's wild."

I stared at Lucas. Didn't he realize what Jody had done? What a great pet Flag was?

"All's I'm saying is sometimes people mean well, but they don't realize what they're getting themselves into. Things get complicated," Lucas continued.

I thought of my own wild animals in the barn, of Lucas and Lindy moving in next door, of all the good things happening that summer.

"But Flag's home is with Jody," I whispered. "They're meant for each other."

Lucas didn't answer; instead we both concentrated on Jax's belly. Clouds of yellow fur rose up around us, and Jax murmured gratefully in that droopy-eyed way dogs do.

"What about you? Do you ever miss home?" I asked finally.

"Home?" Lucas laughed, but stopped when he realized I was serious.

"How come you've moved so much?" I asked. It was a harmless question, but I wished I could take it back. Lucas shifted to his feet, abruptly wiping the dirt from his jeans.

"It's getting late. I better go help with dinner," he said. Something crunched under his sneaker, and he picked up a piece of broken red plastic. "What's this?"

The black car popped into my mind. "Oh, I bet it fell off that car. The taillight was broken."

Lucas flinched. "What car?"

"I don't know," I said. "Some old car. It was parked in your driveway."

"When? Who was in it?" He looked at me like I was hiding something from him.

"Yesterday afternoon. Some strange man, but he left." I pictured the pale-faced driver, the blank look on his face like a washed-out photo.

"What did he say? Did you talk to him?" Lucas's voice was urgent now, his eyes wide with alarm.

"No," I said, wishing he would sit back down, feeling like I'd done something wrong.

"Did he have dark hair?"

I nodded, wondering how Lucas could have guessed. He lurched toward the house, startling Jax.

"Why didn't you tell me, Franny?" There was fear in his voice, and I felt somehow responsible.

Desperately, I reached for Sidda's invitation in my back pocket. I'd give it to him now. It would cheer him up.

But the cabin door banged shut. He was already gone.

County Fair

"What book are you on now?" It was Friday, and Pearl stood on the other side of the screen door, her hair billowing around her like a storm. Jax leaped up and barked at the sight of her.

"Number six," I groaned, letting her in. In the light, Pearl's hair looked like fire, the frizzy flames leaping off her head.

Sidda clapped her hand over her mouth, then stepped forward. "Wow, Pearl, that's quite a look!" She inspected Pearl's hair, hands wringing behind her back. I could tell Sidda was just dying to get a hairbrush.

Pearl shrugged. "Mother's been busy," she explained. "Her garden club is setting up their booth for the big fair tonight, and I can't braid it without help."

"Ooh! Allow me!" Sidda clapped. Unknowing victims and hairstyling opportunities did not often present themselves together, and Sidda disappeared quickly to our room. I imagined her diving into her beauty drawer.

"Hey, Pearl, wanna hold George?" Ben was dangling the turtle dangerously close to Pearl's hair.

"Beat it, Ben! We have work to do." Sidda returned and wedged herself between them in one deft move, wielding her basket of ribbons and brushes like a small army. She surveyed the battlefield, selected her weapon of choice, and pounced on Pearl's hair with a purple comb.

"Ouch!" Pearl yelped.

"Beauty is never pain-free," Sidda said. She looked at me. "Observe one who has never suffered a day in her life."

I ignored this. I was too busy counting the Animal Funds donations in my coffee can. Forty-two dollars and seventeen cents!

"Ready to go to the fair?" I asked. I think Pearl nodded, but it was hard to tell. Sidda was tugging her head up and down with all those brushes.

ooo

Half an hour later, with bows firmly tied in Pearl's red hair, we were whizzing down back roads as Mrs. Jones navigated her "secret route" to the fair. The Grafton County Fair was the highlight of the summer for every kid in town. The fourth week of July a band of trucks rolled up Main Street and into the town park, pulling trailers of rides, game booths, and attractions. It was the one weekend of the year when every kid in Grafton skipped dinner to stand in line, when bedtimes were overlooked and you made every ticket count, weighing with care the choice of a cotton candy or one more ride on the roller coaster.

Pearl and I leaped out of the car before Mrs. Jones had come to a full stop at the entrance gates.

"Now, Pearl, you may ride the merry-go-round and the Ferris wheel. No spinning teacups, no waterslide, and absolutely no bumper cars." We stared at Mrs. Jones. This, coming from the most dangerous driver in town.

"Don't talk to strangers—they kidnap you. And no junk food—it makes you barf. Meet me at the Garden Booth by nine o'clock. We have books at home to read." Mrs. Jones turned her attention to me. "Did Pearl tell you she was on her twelfth book? This could be our summer!" She clapped her pudgy hands together, and in the backseat, baby Mable clapped hers.

"Woof!" barked Mable, as the car spun away from the gates.

"So, which is it?" I asked. "The merry-go-round or the Ferris wheel?"

Pearl straightened Sidda's pink bow in her hair and marched off. "Definitely the bumper cars," she said.

Frog Hop

Well, well, look what fell off the merry-go-round!" Izzy handed us each a chocolate chip cookie in a red, white, and blue napkin. The ladies were working Grandma Rae's bake stand, famous for its homemade pies and donations to the church.

"Come with us to the frog hop?" I asked them.

Ben had entered George and Martha in the competition. Dad tried to explain that there wasn't much hope of either turtle out-hopping the frogs, but Ben argued that reptiles and amphibians were practically cousins, and finally Mama agreed to enter them. The judges had allowed it with amused chuckles, sensing little objection to two slow turtles being entered in a frog hopping contest.

"Ben's trying to beat the Walker frog," I explained.

The ladies gasped.

The Walker family lived on the largest pond in town and were known to bring unusually large and odd-looking frogs to the fair each year. In fact, the Walker boys themselves were a little large and odd-looking.

"Let's go!" Izzy said.

"We are not abandoning our Christian baking booth!" Grandma replied.

"Just watch us," Izzy said, hanging up a Closed sign. "Even God had a rest on the seventh day, Rae. And for all we know, he spent it at the frog hop. Now let's go."

Grandma Rae sputtered as Izzy yanked the awning over the concession stand and the baking booth disappeared behind it.

Pearl and I led the way for the ladies, down the grassy aisles of game booths, giant prizes, and stuffed animals. Kids tossed rings, fired plastic guns, and threw balls. I scanned the crowd for Lucas. Once, I thought I heard someone call out my name, but the crowd pulled us forward. Past the booths, the field opened up into the rides, a glowing circus against the late-day sun. Little kids sailed by on the merry-go-round, the painted horses surging up and down on their candy-colored poles. I spotted Sidda and her girlfriends in the bumper car line, giggling and pointing at boys in cars. In the distance, the Ferris wheel rolled into the sky, the top seats tipping gently against the clouds.

"Will you look at that. I always feel young when I see the Ferris wheel," Izzy said, draping her arm around me.

The frog hop was set up at the north end of the field. It was a small grassy pen with individually roped-off lanes, but the crowd surrounding it was large. Mama and Lindy waved us over to Ben's lane, where Ben and Daddy were positioning the turtles.

"Have you seen the competition?" Mama asked.

He was the ugliest frog any of us had ever laid eyes on. Longer and bumpier than all the rest, the Walker frog towered over his opponents, his bulging eyes half-closed like he'd just finished a big meal. Jeb Walker's own bulging eyes also rested half-closed, but I don't think he could help that. The lane beside the Walker frog was empty.

"I think it ate the competition," Dotty whispered.

Silence settled over the pen, and the announcer stepped forward. "On your marks, get set, go!"

A horn blew and the crowd went wild. Frogs flew forward and back, zigzagging across lanes, and sometimes into the crowd. Lindy and Mama cheered loudly. Pearl covered her eyes.

"Go, George! Go, Martha!" Ben hollered. As if in response, the turtles pulled their heads into their shells and disappeared.

Before we knew it the horn blew again, and Jeb Walker scooped up his winner at the finish line, waving him around for everyone to see.

"Poor Ben," Izzy said with a sigh.

"Don't worry, that was just the first heat," Mama assured her. "There are three more throughout the night." But the rest of us didn't share her hope.

"We'll check in later," I promised Mama. "Tell Ben good luck."

"Back to the booth," Grandma ordered, rounding up the ladies.

"Did Lucas give you a free try at the ring toss?" Lindy asked me.

Suddenly I remembered hearing my name in the crowd.

"He's here?" I asked her.

"At Harland's ring toss stand. It's their annual booth."

I fingered the invitation in my pocket. I hadn't seen Lucas since I'd told him about the car. I'd been carrying it around for the last three days, hoping to see him, glad for the excuse to talk to him. I couldn't stand the thought of him still being mad.

"Let's go," I told Pearl.

Teenagers gathered around the ring toss, mostly girls, I noticed. And there, smack-dab in the middle, was Sidda. I pushed my way to the front.

"Win anything?" I asked her.

She frowned. "These games are for *kids*." As she said it, Lucas tossed me a ring.

"Hey, Franny! Try your luck."

I studied his face. He certainly didn't look mad.

"Lucas, are you coming to my party?" Marilee asked him.

My stomach fell.

"What party?" he asked.

"My birthday, tomorrow. Didn't you get the invitation?" She looked at Sidda, who glared at me.

"We sent you an invitation," Sidda said, her eyes still on me. "I can't understand what could have happened to it."

I covered my pocket with my hand and looked away. It was too late to offer it now.

"What time do you finish, Lucas?" Sidda asked, turning her attention back to him.

"Eight o'clock," he said, glancing at the ring still in my hand. "Go on, Franny, give it a shot."

I aimed and tossed, holding my breath as the ring hurtled through the air like a Frisbee, skimming the top of a blue bottle before it hit the curtain behind it.

"Missed!" yelled Marilee.

I felt my face flush.

"Try again," Lucas said, handing me two more. The second one bounced off the top of a pink bottle, looped around it twice, then spun off.

"Almost," Pearl whispered beside me.

I felt braver as I held the last ring.

Sidda hauled her pink purse onto the table next to me. "Here, Lucas, I think I have an extra invite somewhere." She fished around in her bag and retrieved a purple envelope. "I hope you can make the party, on *such short notice*."

I could feel her hard stare.

"Thanks," he said, opening it eagerly. "Sounds like fun."

My face burned.

"By the way," Sidda added, "we're all meeting at the Ferris wheel at nine. You should come."

I felt the baby wolf flick its tail inside me. I think it may have even growled. This time I tossed the ring hard. It hit the back curtain and dropped, right onto a green bottle.

"Fifty points!" yelled Pearl, jumping up and down. I spun around to see Lucas's reaction.

But he wasn't watching. He was reading the invitation, a wide smile on his face.

Ferris Wheel

"I don't even like corn dogs," Pearl whined.

It was almost nine o'clock and Pearl and I were in the corn dog line, which just happened to be next to the Ferris wheel. I tossed Sidda's invitation in the trash. What would Lucas think if he knew I'd kept it from him?

"And Mother says they're full of preservatives," Pearl added with a cringe. "I don't want to stunt my growth."

"Just eat it," I said, handing the vendor my money and passing Pearl a dog. Sometimes Pearl was so clueless.

"I know why we're here," she said, eyeing me over her untouched corn dog. Okay, maybe not clueless, but definitely annoying.

"Pass the ketchup," a gravelly voice said. Standing beside

me at the condiment table was the pale-faced man from the driveway. I stared as he took the bottle from my hand, emptying all that remained onto his corn dog.

I nudged Pearl, and we moved aside. "I know that man," I whispered. "He was at Lucas's the other day."

The man tore off a large bite, staring into the crowd. I shivered. I remembered all the questions Lucas had asked about this man, and how upset he'd been when I couldn't answer them.

"Let's move," Pearl suggested. "He's creepy."

She was right, but I couldn't leave. Now was my chance to make it up to Lucas. I turned back to him.

"Excuse me, sir. Do you remember me?" The pale-faced man scowled down at us, saying nothing. I concentrated on his ketchup-smeared lips. "I saw you a few days ago. Outside my neighbor's house."

He stopped chewing, wiped the arm of his jacket hastily across his mouth. His stare grew colder, not kinder, and I stiffened.

"You were in the Dunns' driveway, in your car," I reminded him.

His eyes flashed, a quick, crooked smile passing over his face. "The Dunns," he said and chuckled. "So I did have the right house."

Suddenly this didn't seem like a good idea anymore. Pearl tugged on my sleeve.

"Well, well, well." He laughed again, tossing his unfinished corn dog in the garbage can. "Thanks, kid. You just saved me a lot of trouble."

Pearl tugged harder. I turned to see Lucas heading our way through the crowd.

"Lucas!" I called, pointing frantically to the man behind me. But when I turned back around, the man was already gone.

"So people really eat those things?" Lucas asked, eyeing our corn dogs.

Pearl piped up, "Franny sure does. She suddenly developed quite an appetite for them."

I elbowed her, searching the crowd. But the man had truly disappeared. Had he seen Lucas? Wasn't that what he'd wanted?

"Want to ride the Ferris wheel?" Lucas asked, interrupting my worries.

I looked over my shoulder once more to where the man had been standing, then back at Lucas's bright smile. I didn't want anything to ruin this moment. What difference would it make if I told him about the man later?

We were almost at the front of the Ferris wheel line when I felt a tap on my shoulder.

"How nice of you to hold our place!" It was Sidda, googly-eyed and grinning, with Marilee and their friend Beth giggling beside her. Honestly, I couldn't imagine what they thought was so secret and so funny all the time. "I'm afraid I'm out of tickets," she said, pouting dramatically. "Franny, you'll give me yours, won't you?"

I stared at her in disbelief. "But I only have enough for this ride," I objected.

Sidda shrugged. Clearly, this did not concern her. She held out her hand and waited.

"Take these," Lucas offered, digging in his pocket. He

placed a crumpled handful of tickets in her open palm. "I get extras for working at the fair."

"Wow, thanks," Sidda said, stuffing the tickets in her purse, offering none to the rest of us. We were at the front of the line now. A giant yellow seat swung slowly down, and the Ferris wheel operator steadied it. It was the last empty one.

"Who's next?" the operator called.

"We are!" Sidda shouted, pushing me aside to stand by Lucas. She hopped into the empty seat, and her friends piled in beside her.

My heart sank.

"Oh, Lucas! There's room next to me," Sidda hollered, shoving Marilee over.

There was a pause, and the ride operator looked impatient.

"Oh, no!" Pearl cried beside me. "It's nine. I have to meet my mother." She dashed off into the crowd, leaving me alone. *What now?* I wondered.

"Come on, Lucas!" Sidda cried.

"Go ahead," Lucas answered. "I'll catch the next one with Franny."

My heart pounded. The look on Sidda's face was enough to freeze the Ferris wheel, to stop every ride and game in time, but it was too late. The ride operator clicked the safety bar closed, and Sidda swung into the night, her legs kicking and her mouth moving silently up, up, up, into the sky.

"I think she wanted to ride with you," I told Lucas.

"But I wanted to ride with you." He smiled down at me, and my legs felt fuzzy. It didn't matter that we had to wait ten minutes for a turn. Lucas sat right next to me, our knees pressing together, as the wheel turned and lifted us into the sky.

"Look how tiny everyone looks," I said. From the top of the Ferris wheel the town shimmered with the glow of games and lights and the purple shadows of kids moving through the park. Yet I felt safe and cozy, the thrill of the distance from the ground no match for the thrill of Lucas Dunn seated beside me.

"Makes you want to stay up here awhile, doesn't it?" he said. And then he reached over and put his hand on mine, right on the bar in front of us. My head swam. I thought of the animal patients nestled safely in my barn and of the throbbing chirp of the peepers in the riverbed below our yard. Summer to my hands, my eyes, my ears. I closed my eyes, my body filling with the gentle pull of the wheel, the swaying of the chair, the night air lifting around us. I felt myself fill up, spill over into the sky, the summer fever quivering in my bones. I squeezed Lucas's hand. I wanted him to know, to feel what I felt.

And then the ride slowed, the Ferris wheel stopped to let people off. It delivered us down into the crowd, returning us to the regular noise of the world, the spell of the starry night hovering above us like a promise.

Homecoming

"We did it! We beat the Walker frog!" Ben yelled.

"How?" I asked. We were walking home through the quiet streets with Lindy and Lucas, slowed by bellies full of carnival food. Ben bounced on Dad's shoulders, a cotton candy in one fist and his frog trophy in the other.

"Well, most of the competition jumped into the crowd, so the only real threat was the Walker frog." Ben was completely wound up. "He's big, but not so smart. He took one big hop, then stopped. When Martha saw that frog ahead of her in the lane, she just pulled her head out and started following. And when Martha went, George went. The Walker frog was just one hop away from the finish line, and here comes Martha running up behind him—"

"Martha ran?" I asked.

Mama winked.

"Yes!" Ben shouted. "And so here she comes running, and the Walker frog is just about to take his last hop, and all of a sudden his big bulgy eyes get real sleepy-looking, and they start to close, and *conk*, he just falls asleep. Right there on the track."

"He fell asleep?" Lucas asked, breaking into laughter.

"Like a baby," Ben said. He hugged his frog trophy to his chest, his face covered in pink cotton candy.

"Jeb Walker falls asleep in school all the time," Sidda said.

"Well, there you go," said Dad.

We cut through the Dorsens' pasture, newly mowed, and climbed Berry Hill, taking the shortcut home. It was a beautiful night for a walk. We were all having such a fine time celebrating the frog hop and the fair, laughing so loud, that no one noticed the rusty black car parked in Lindy's driveway when we arrived home. The same car from the other day.

"Looks like you've got company," Dad said.

Lindy halted, wrapping her shawl tightly around her shoulders. We all peered into the darkness, wondering who was there.

Except for Lucas and Lindy. They seemed to know.

Mama stepped forward, her hand moving to touch Lindy's arm. "Are you all right?" she asked.

Lindy didn't look so good. There was a creak on the porch. The pale-faced man stood up from one of the rocking chairs, rising from the darkness like a spooky moon, right there on Lindy's porch. He stared at us, saying nothing.

"Who is that?" Ben asked.

Lindy's voice quivered. "That's Lucas's father," she said.

The Uninvited Guest

The cabin was quiet the next morning. It stayed quiet all weekend. The potting shed doors remain closed, and Jax whined at the edge of the yard with a stick in his mouth. On Sunday morning, Sidda complained that Lucas had never shown up at Marilee's party on Saturday night.

"Something's not right," Mama said, clutching her coffee mug at the breakfast table. "Did you see the look on Lindy's face the other night?"

We'd said good night after finding Mr. Dunn on Lindy's porch. I could tell Mama didn't want to leave her. It was like all the beauty of our night had been sucked up into the cloudless sky, a storm of worry in its place.

I wanted to tell my parents what Lucas had told me about his father that day in the barn. I felt betrayed. Dead fathers don't show up in cars or eat corn dogs at fairs. But first, I wanted to ask him about it myself.

"I'm inviting the Dunns for dinner," Mama said, getting up and gathering her cookbooks. When anything went wrong, Mama liked to get everyone around the dining room table. I could see the hairs of the mother wolf rising on her neck as she paced the kitchen.

Dad saw it, too. "Now, Celia, maybe we should give them some time to visit. I'm sure everything's just fine," he assured her.

But the mother wolf was stubborn. "Then a dinner invitation will give us a chance to meet him," she insisted.

But we never did. Mama called the cabin, and the phone rang and rang before Lindy answered. She thanked Mama but said they couldn't come. This just made Mama more worried and she spent the rest of the day at her easel, glaring at the old woman in her painting, prodding her angrily with the brushes.

"Who is that?" I asked, examining the painted woman, the familiar straight line of her back, the determined jaw.

But Mama didn't answer. She abandoned her paints and stared out the window at the little cabin.

"You can't drag them over here," Dad said, but I had a feeling that was exactly what Mama would do if she could.

I was just as curious. I don't know if that's because we are as alike as Grandma Rae says or because of what Lucas had told me in the barn that day. But I took on my own mission and began spying on the cabin.

Cooling Off

"Girls, girls, girls. Less talk, more books."

Pearl and I looked up at the giant shadow looming over us, blocking out the sun.

"Where is it, Pearl?" Mrs. Jones asked.

"Right here, Mother." Pearl slid Nancy Drew number 5 out from under her towel.

"Well, what good is it doing under there? Hand over that ice cream. You need to focus." Mrs. Jones whisked the half-eaten cone from Pearl's sticky hand and headed back toward the pool, where Pearl's little brothers were trying to drown each other.

Pearl sank onto her towel.

"We can share," I said, passing her my ice cream.

It was the end of July. There were just a few weeks left in the Aubree Library summer reading contest, and Pearl was not making much progress. Oh, she was enjoying her books. And that seemed like enough to me. But not to Mrs. Jones. As far as she was concerned, that gold trophy gleaming in her living room window would be the only proof of any progress.

"Let's take a dip," I said. It was another scorcher, the Monday of what promised to be another rainless week, and it appeared the whole town was squeezed in the pool. I swirled my feet in the water and lowered myself in with a sigh. The weekend was over, and with it the fair, and I wondered idly if

Lucas was working at Harland's today or still at home with his father. I wanted desperately to see him.

"Pearl, what page are you on?" Mrs. Jones demanded. That woman had ears like radar. She peered at us in the shallow end, where two of Pearl's little brothers bobbed up and down. She was just lowering herself into the water with Mable when the oldest Jones boy cannonballed off the pool deck and over her head. Mrs. Jones screamed as a wave of water crashed over us, but we didn't have time to laugh.

Suddenly, above Mrs. Jones's scream, there was another: a long, shrill wail that echoed across the pool, silencing everyone, even the Jones boys themselves. We covered our ears. It was the fire whistle. Two red trucks rounded the corner, their sirens blasting. Behind them an ambulance followed, and behind that another fire truck.

"What's going on?" Pearl shouted.

The pool emptied quickly as people lined up by the fence to watch. The sirens continued, and a black cloud of smoke filled the sky, rolling lazily toward us.

As usual, there was no room in the red convertible for all of us. Mrs. Jones packed the baby and boys in, crushing one raft and two sand pails as she slammed the trunk shut.

"Come right home," she ordered Pearl, squeezing behind the wheel. By then, the black clouds had risen over the treetops, shadowing the parking lot.

We wrapped our towels around our waists and walked fast, past the ball fields and the school. Past the park where the fair had just been. Above us, the smoke grew thicker in the sky, and the odor of charcoal filled our noses.

"Where do you think it's coming from?" I asked.

A small crowd had gathered on the steps of the library.

"It's the orchard," a woman said. "The whole thing's gone up!"

Pearl and I exchanged looks. Blue Jay's Orchard was on the edge of town, just a couple miles from my house. It was a place we knew well. Any blueberry tart or apple pie in town was made with fruit from Blue Jay's. Suddenly, all I could think of was home, Mama, and my barn, with its patients closed inside.

"I've gotta go," I said to Pearl and took off, leaving her on the sidewalk.

Ruins

"Woe is me," Grandma Rae whispered the next afternoon.

We'd come to see for ourselves. The charcoal fields stretched out before us up and down the Cimarron Throughway. Even the dirt was burned. Black sticks rose out of the ground, row after row of smoking tree skeletons.

"Scary," Ben whispered, squeezing my hand.

Up and down the road, families pulled over to look. It was the saddest summer attraction. Only the little red road stand sign remained, a smiley-faced apple on dancing legs. "Welcome to Blue Jay's Orchard!" he greeted the crowd.

"Poor, poor Emma," Grandma said, glancing over at her friend. "I'd better go see her."

Not far away was old Emma Johnson herself, the owner of Blue Jay's Orchard, slumped on the tailgate of a pickup truck.

The fire marshal patted her back, and said something we couldn't hear. It didn't matter. No words could make a difference now.

"It's what we all feared," Mama said, turning for home. Her eyes watered as she spoke, and she wiped at them quickly.

"Got smoke in your eyes?" Ben asked, reaching up to pat Mama.

"Just woe," she responded.

The grass was burned right up to the roadside. I kicked at the dirt, digging my toe into its crusted layers. A small pebble rolled free. Smooth and white, no bigger than a robin's egg, it tumbled across the charred ground untouched by the flames that had roared over it. I picked it up. Some things are like that, I guess. Even as flames lick the surface above, some things get tucked away safely, only to be unearthed just as pure and lovely as before. A little piece of snow-white hope in a scorched field.

"How bad is it?" Daddy asked us when he got home that evening. We'd plopped ourselves on the porch, exhausted by what we'd just seen, wondering who would be next.

"It's all gone," Mama told him, shaking her head sadly.

Sidda joined us on the porch. "No cider doughnuts this fall?" she asked.

"Or fresh apples," Mama said. We sat on the porch a long time, thinking of the seasons we'd spent at Blue Jay's. The Halloween parade among the trees, the apple-picking afternoons and sticky cider lips. The Johnsons had lost their farm. And with it we'd lost a part of ourselves. Ben whimpered a little and climbed into Dad's lap.

"I need a tissue," Ben cried. "I've got woe in my eyes."

Hospital

After the orchard burned, it became official. There was an emergency town meeting that Tuesday night, and the water restrictions were upgraded to a full ban.

"Save the water for the fields and livestock," people said.

When the president of the garden club had the nerve to water his prize roses, Grandma Rae almost ran him over with her town car.

The summer fever hit us hard, and it wasn't in the moony-eyed July way we were used to. The animal hospital was bursting. With everyone out walking their fields and inspecting their pastures, the whole town's eyes were on the ground. And that made for all kinds of discoveries. Ruby Miller, one of Grandma's church friends, found a nest of three baby opossums curled in her shed that Wednesday morning, and by lunchtime five-year-old Melody Watson was knocking on our door with a frog in her hand.

"Bob's thirsty," she said.

Ben took one look at that curly-haired little girl holding a frog named Bob and it was true love. "He needs a bath," he told her.

Melody looked offended. "Bob's not dirty. He's just thirsty."

"That's how it works," Ben explained. "He soaks up water with his skin."

The way Melody looked at him, he might as well have told

her that the frog had landed from the moon. But she followed him to the barn and giggled as Bob got his bath. Afterward, she even donated two nickels to our coffee can.

"For heaven's sake," Grandma Rae said, stepping over the food bottles and trays and buckets that lined our porch. "The critters have taken over."

I had to admit she was right. As it was we were running back and forth to the barn day and night. The stalls were full and noisy, and the old patients were being pushed aside by the new. We were so busy I barely had time to think, but still I looked for Lucas. I wanted to introduce him to the new patients.

"The time is coming," Mama told me that night as she tucked me in.

"I know," I said, sliding under my sheets. She was talking about the swallows.

"They'll be fine," she said, pressing her lips to my forehead. "You did real good."

I dreamed of my swallow babies that night, soaring into the stars above my house and the cabin next door. Circling over burned fields, gliding farther and farther away. But flying home again. Always coming home.

Potting Shed

On Thursday morning, the doors to the potting shed were open. Jax saw it first and bounded off the porch in search of Lucas.

I found Mama staring at the woman in her painting. She set her paints down right away. We stopped at the garden to fill a basket and made our way next door.

"Lindy, may we come in?" Mama asked, peering into the dark shed.

Lindy was seated behind her wheel, her apron splattered with fresh wet clay. She smiled when she saw us in the door, but it was different. Her eyes didn't crinkle at the edges.

"We've missed you this week," Mama said, setting down a basket of corn and beans. "Thought you might like these."

Lindy wiped her hands on a fresh towel. "They're beautiful, thank you," she said, bending over the basket. A faint breeze stirred in the doorway, the first breeze any of us had felt in a long time, and we all turned our faces to greet it.

"A lot has happened," Mama said.

"Yes," said Lindy. I wasn't sure if she was referring to the orchard fire that week or the arrival of Mr. Dunn. It seemed the torrent of events had stretched the week so thin it languished, unable to move itself forward.

Our silent questions filled the potting shed, and Lindy didn't try to swat them away. "Been busy." She shrugged, pointing to the boxes of pottery on the kiln. "I've gotten behind on my work since Carl came."

"Is that his name?" Mama's voice was soft and curious, the way it is when she speaks to a child or a small animal.

"Yes. I'm sorry you haven't met him yet. His arrival was, well . . . unexpected."

Mama nodded as if she understood, but I didn't see how

she could. I didn't want her nodding at Lindy that way. I wanted Lindy to go on. There was more to tell, I knew.

"How are you?" Mama asked. Waiting for an answer, she lowered herself quietly onto a bench by the window. Mama reached over and pulled a daisy from the basket, turning it over in her hands, patiently. Not knowing what to do with myself, I sat next to her.

Lindy didn't answer right away. But Mama nodded anyway, turning the flower over and over in her fingers. She hummed a little as Lindy bent over her wheel. They sat like that awhile.

It was then I heard it. It was a silent language, rising and falling between them. I had seen this before, in the rare quiet moments of the sewing circle, in the way Grandma Rae rested her hand on a sad shoulder at church, in the gentle way a woman in the grocery store meets the eyes of a young mother with a crying baby. The gestures were soft and silent. Yet from them swelled a presence warm and thick in the room, a safe haven for secrets or confessions, fears and truths.

Lindy's hands returned to the wet clay, working the round ball more assuredly as the wheel picked up speed.

"I'll be fine," Lindy said finally.

Will be, not *am*, I noted. The wheel spun faster, and the ball took shape under her fingers as they danced around it.

"And Lucas?" Mama asked.

"Lucas is okay." As soon as she said it, Lindy shook her head. "Actually, that's not really true, but I think it's just teenage stuff. He and his father, well . . ." She stopped then, a strangled hiccup escaping her throat.

Mama returned the daisy to the vegetable basket, rose and crossed the small shed to Lindy, and laid her hand on Lindy's arm. The wheel slowed to a stop, the clay went still under her hands, and Lindy looked at Mama.

"If you need anything," Mama whispered.

Lindy nodded, wiping the back of her hand quickly across her face, a trail of red clay in its wet path.

Mama's work was done. She motioned for me to come, and I hopped up quickly, seemingly forgotten but not. We left the shed then, crossing our yard, where Mama draped her arm around me. We did not talk. I wasn't sure what I had just seen or heard, but I felt the weight of what passed between Mama and Lindy heavy in the air around us. Behind us, the potting shed hummed, the little wheel turning once again.

Night Noises

"Where's Lucas?" It was Ben who asked, at dinner that night. He stuffed a Brussels sprout in his mouth and looked at us.

"Who cares?" Sidda said, pushing her fork around her plate. Since the fair and Marilee's party, Sidda had shown a sudden change of heart toward Lucas Dunn.

"He's visiting with his father," Dad said.

Mama forced a smile.

"I seen that man," Ben said, turning the Brussels sprout over and over in his mouth, as though trying to remember if this was one of the vegetables he liked or not.

"Where?" I asked.

"I was in the barn."

"No, where'd you see *him*?"

"Oh. He was in Lindy's potting shed tonight. He's a real clumsy man."

Sidda frowned. "Why do you say that?"

"Because of the noise. I was in the barn when I heard it. There was a big crash and then another one, and then he came outside with a box of Lindy's pots. All smashed up. Lindy cried, but he wouldn't let her touch them."

Mama looked at Daddy then, her face dark and serious.

"Well, maybe Mr. Dunn didn't want Lindy to hurt herself on the broken pots. Maybe he was putting them in a safe place," Mama said, but I could tell she didn't believe this.

"No," Ben said. "He just threw them in the river."

Our river, outside our house. Just fifty steps away from our dinner table. I imagined Lindy's shattered pots, glimmering on the riverbed under the stars.

"Did that man see you?" Mama asked.

"No, I was feeding Speed Bump. She was real hungry. She ate thirteen worms!"

Dad patted Ben's hand. "That's great, honey. You're taking good care of her." He put his fork down and looked at us. "I want you kids to stay away from the Dunn house for now. I don't want you going anywhere near there, understand?"

I looked at Mama, who was nodding.

"But why?" I asked, thinking of Lindy in her shed, her worried eyes and her sad laugh.

"Because it's not a good time right now. Daddy and I will take care of this. Just promise us, all right?" Mama said. Her eyes locked on mine.

I couldn't imagine staying away from them. But the look on Mama's face filled my tummy with worry, so I promised her I would.

Catching Lucas

That night, after dinner, I planted myself on the porch swing with the opossums. I may have promised not to go to Lucas's house, but I hadn't promised not to see him at mine. I was tired of waiting. It had only been a few days since the fair, but they were urgent ones, filled with need and worry, drought and fire. And something else. Something dark and troublesome coming from his cabin across the way.

At night, I no longer drifted to sleep to the sounds of the potting shed humming, but to something else. The cold chink of a beer bottle being set on a porch floor. Bottle after bottle, until I lost count and fell into slumber. Each morning, there was a long row on the railing, glass soldiers lined up that Lindy swept quickly into a garbage bag. For a homecoming, none of the Dunns looked too happy.

So while Daddy had forbidden me to visit him, I wished Lucas to visit me. It didn't take long. I was rocking the opossums, wishing hard, when the cabin door opened.

"Lucas!" I hissed into the darkness.

He froze.

Come here, I motioned.

He hesitated, looking back at the cabin. Then, as if making up his mind, he hurried over.

"Where've you been?" I asked.

"Busy," he said, stepping deftly around the question like it was a gaping hole in my yard. The way Lindy had done earlier.

"Look," I said. I unwrapped the opossum pouch just enough so a pink nose stuck out.

Lucas climbed hesitantly up the porch stairs. "Wow, where'd you find these guys?" he asked, moving closer.

"Ruby Miller brought them over. She's a friend of Grandma Rae's."

Lucas sat down beside me on the swing. "They're neat," he said quietly.

"Mama helped me sew them a flannel pouch from one of Dad's old shirts."

Lucas grinned at it. "It's like a little opossum sleeping bag."

"Want to hold them?" I asked. I was hungry for him to stay, to talk to me. I held the pouch out to him like an offering. Relief filled me when he reached for it.

Lucas took the bag gently and cradled it against him. It was real natural, not like you'd expect from a boy. "They're warm," he said.

I watched him carefully, trying to ignore the questions banging around in my brain like fireflies in a mason jar. *He's back,* my heart sang.

We sat like that awhile, listening to the peepers. When Lucas didn't say much, I did. I filled the strange emptiness around us, plucking every funny or sad detail I could think of out of the last few days, until the cold worry that was between us was crowded and colored with the life of it all. I told him about the new patients I'd gotten, how Pearl and I had run home from the pool under the smoke that Monday, how the black skeletons of the orchard trees reached eerily up to the sky.

As I talked, I could feel him relax on the seat next to me, a warmth that spread through the wood and into my own limbs. The tight corners of his mouth unraveled.

"He found us," he said, finally.

"But you said . . ."

"I know what I said." He sighed.

I stiffened. Lucas had lied to me.

"He's no good around us," he said, softly.

Suddenly it became clear to me. Their few belongings, the places they'd moved from, the freshly painted name wiped off their mailbox. Lucas and Lindy did not want to be found. "You're not moving again, are you?" I asked, afraid already of the answer.

"I don't know. We don't have enough money to go anywhere just yet," he said.

There were so many things I wanted to ask, but I didn't want to scare him off the porch, away from our yard again. "My family's worried about you and your mama," I whispered.

"Well, tell them don't be. I'm going to take care of it. Soon."

The cabin's screen door swung open, and Lucas jerked beside me.

"I've gotta go," he said. Quickly, he passed me the opossums. As he did, his sleeve caught on the porch swing. It rolled up over his forearm, his warm skin brushing against my own. He gasped.

I looked before he could cover what I saw. A blue trail of bruises wrapping around his wrist, purple blotches rising off his skin. "Lucas!" I cried.

He jerked his shirtsleeve down. "Don't," he warned, his voice angry at first. Then, softly, "Please don't." And then he disappeared into the twilight.

"I won't," I promised the empty seat beside me. And so I sat, shaking on the swing. It was worse than I'd thought, worse than I'd ever imagined.

Just beyond the porch, Sidda's voice poured through our open bedroom window. Through the screen door, I could hear Ben's giggles as Dad read him a story in the family room. It seemed impossible. Two houses side by side along the same bubbling river: one brimming with warm voices that spilled from its windows, one aching with a sadness that rippled from its shingled roof like rainwater.

Don't, he'd said.

Don't what? Don't ask questions? Don't tell what I'd seen? My stomach churned. It didn't matter which he meant. I already knew; it was a promise I couldn't keep for long.

Busy Bodies

"Where's that firecracker of a friend of yours?" Izzy asked Mama. She lifted a blue square from the table, setting it into place in the quilted sky.

Mama sighed and walked from her easel to the window, the gray eyes of her painted lady following her warily. A hot gloom had settled over the Friday Bee. Mama yanked open the windows, but that just seemed to let more heat in. The curtains rested quietly against them, not even the faintest breeze to stir the air.

"Is Lindy ill?" Grandma asked, watching Mama over the rims of her eyeglasses.

"No. Just not around lately," Mama replied.

Izzy met Mama's eyes, and the look that passed between them took me back to the kitchen, back to Izzy's words. *A river of sadness, that one.*

"Well, come sit," Grandma scolded Mama. "You've been pacing around here like a cat in a room full of rockers. You're making me nervous."

Mama joined the women at the table, taking a seat by Dotty, who gave her a little pat.

Grandma eyed me. "Aren't you sewing with us? You could use the practice."

I shook my head, busily counting the Animal Funds. Sixty-three dollars, after the formula and seeds Daddy had picked up at the pet store for me. "Have to feed the new opossums," I told her. "Your friend Ruby brought them. Found them behind the church."

"Opossums?" Grandma Rae asked, her mouth twisting in distaste. "Ruby Miller did that?"

"Churchgoing opossums," Ben told her. "And they play dead, too!" He rolled over on the rug, legs up in the air to demonstrate.

"Oh, they're something," Izzy said, dropping a dollar in my can. "Clever little devils, playing dead like that. Think people would leave me alone if I rolled over on the ground?"

"Really now," Grandma said, but everyone else laughed. They were still laughing when Faye Wakeman lumbered in, red and stooped.

"Faye," Mama said. "Are you all right?"

We watched as Faye plunked down in her rightful chair by Grandma.

"Just a hot spell. Been up since dawn trying to get some water on the corn. Nothing left in the river."

"I heard the Dorsen farm closed for the season. Their sorghum crop dried up," Dotty said.

Grandma sent her a warning look, and Dotty covered her mouth. "Oh, Faye, I'm sorry. I didn't mean . . ."

"No, no," Faye piped up, taking the iced tea Mama offered her. "There's no getting around it. We're all hurting bad. We've applied for state aid, but I don't know how much we'll get."

Everyone, it seemed, was applying for government aid. I'd seen the state trucks driving up and down the town roads, out to inspect the fields for crop yield. It was only early August, and the month's harvests were already being declared lost. Faye was right, everyone was hurting bad.

Izzy winked at me. "Isn't it about time to feed those critters?"

I nodded, glad for an excuse to leave the sad group.

"Sidda, you and Ben give Franny a hand," Mama suggested. For once Sidda didn't argue. Clearly the ladies needed to talk.

In the kitchen, we gathered the new formula from the fridge and pulled clean bottles out of the dishwasher. I held the tray steady while Ben and Sidda piled supplies onto it. I was almost out the front door when loud voices erupted from the yard.

I looked up and saw Lucas jump off the porch, followed by his father. He was yelling something at him. But Lucas kept walking.

"What's all that scuffle?" Grandma Rae asked, coming up behind me.

At that moment Lindy emerged. I couldn't hear her, but it seemed like she was trying to get Lucas to come back. His father put his hand out, motioning for her to stop. Then he hollered after Lucas. "Get back here, boy!" Lucas continued to the truck.

"Please," Lindy called from the porch. "Just let him go."

But Carl Dunn didn't. He lunged forward, grabbing Lucas by his arm, twisting it behind him. When Lucas cried out, I dropped my tray, the bottles crashing all around me.

Suddenly, Mama was there. "Franny, get back inside," she cried. She pulled me in, stepping right over the bottles and spilled formula, her voice firm and frightened. The ladies crowded behind us, faces full of alarm.

"Close the door," Dotty yelled.

"I'm calling the police," Izzy said.

"Just wait," Grandma said shakily, her stern voice ruffled by the effort to keep steady. "It's not our business. It could just be a family squabble."

"No," Mama said, swinging the door wide open. "Lindy and Lucas are our business. I'm going over there." The back of the mother wolf arched inside her. She looked over her shoulder once, at Sidda and Ben and me. "Stay here," she told us, the gold flickering in her eyes.

We huddled by the windows, watching as Mama strode off the porch to the driveway.

"Lindy?" she called in a calm voice. "Is everything all right?"

The scene before us shifted as Mama entered it. Lucas's father let go of his arm, and Lucas fell against the truck. Lindy straightened her shirt and wiped the stray hairs from her face as if rearranging the scene before us.

"Oh, Celia, I'm sorry if we disturbed you. Everything's fine, we're fine," Lindy said.

Mama stopped on the edge of the driveway. "Lucas? Are you all right?"

Lucas turned away, leaning against the truck door.

His father spoke instead. "Mrs. Parker?" He moved

toward Mama, brushing himself off, and extending his hand. As he got closer, we could see the forced smile, crooked on his face. "We haven't met."

Mama crossed her arms. "No, we haven't," she said, her shoulders squared.

"Call me Carl. I'm real sorry if we disturbed you. Lucas and his mother are just having a disagreement, is all. Teenagers, you know how it is."

Mama didn't answer him. She looked over his shoulder at Lucas and Lindy. "We've never known Lucas to have any such trouble. Until now."

Carl Dunn stared at Mama, his hands twitching just a little at his sides.

Grandma Rae left the window, clucking her tongue. Izzy squeezed my shoulder. I thought of the phone in the kitchen.

"Mrs. Parker, like I said, it's just a small argument. You don't need to concern yourself with it," Carl Dunn continued.

"Well, I *am* concerned. I want you to know that. And if I have to, I also want you to know I will call the authorities."

Carl Dunn's crooked smile faded and he tipped slightly back as if Mama had hit him. His hands balled into fists, but Mama didn't move.

"Children, come away from that window," Grandma ordered.

Sidda and Ben hurried over to her, but I couldn't. I looked out at Lucas slumped against the truck, at Lindy, who'd moved to him, her arm wrapped around his. Carl Dunn was lying: this wasn't their fight.

With that, it ended. Carl Dunn turned on his heels. Mama stayed in the driveway watching him, the tail of the wolf swishing the dust. Lindy waved timidly and followed him into the house. Lucas grabbed his bike and tore off down the driveway.

When Mama finally came inside, everyone collapsed in their chairs, not one of us speaking. The fierceness had left Mama's face and she rested her head in her hands. Sidda bent beside me, collecting the bottles I'd spilled on the porch.

"That was brave," Izzy said to Mama.

But Grandma Rae shook her head. "It was foolish! Your children were right here, watching."

Mama looked up at us, wiping the dust from her cheeks. The flickering gold had left her eyes. "I know," she said. "That's why I had to do it."

Missing

"He's gone," Lindy cried in our doorway the next evening, her blond hair wild about her face.

"What do you mean?" Mama asked, gently pulling her inside.

"Lucas. I've looked everywhere. In the shed, behind the house, even up in the hills. He's really gone this time."

"What happened?"

"He took his bike to work yesterday afternoon, for his Friday evening shift at Harland's. But he never came home last night." Lindy touched her face. It was then I saw the red mark on her cheek. "It's my fault."

Mama's eyes flashed. "We have to report this."

"No!" Lindy cried, grabbing both of Mama's hands. "I don't want the police."

Mama shook her head. "You need them."

But there was more. "They've already come, Celia. Harland's was robbed last night. They think Lucas did it."

"Robbed?"

"Three thousand dollars, gone. They came by late last night, and told me Lucas didn't show up for work yesterday. Then, sometime during the evening, the store was robbed." Lindy paused, swiping at her tears. "I thought Lucas just needed some time to cool off, but when he didn't come home last night, I knew something was wrong. And now this. Please, we've got to find him."

Lindy was begging, and I couldn't stand it. I ached for Mama to give her whatever it was she wanted.

Mama turned, suddenly remembering us. "Franny, Sidda, take Ben outside," she ordered.

The three of us settled in the grass by the porch, straining to hear. I plucked at the dry blades as we listened, and little golden piles grew around me. I thought of the yearling, caught between the wild and a family, not really belonging to either. Lucas had been right. He knew not because he'd read the book but because he, too, was caught.

"Do you think he stole the money?" Sidda asked.

I looked at the flower chain she was making, the yellow and purple petals wound safely together. If she had asked me that a week ago I would've clobbered her. Now I wasn't so sure. If he had, it was for a good reason. Did that still make him a thief? "He needs help," I told her.

Sidda nodded, and handed me a yellow buttercup. Suddenly I ached to tell her everything: about Lucas's arm, the lie about his father, and what he'd made me promise. Dad's truck pulled into the driveway, and Ben jumped up, racing alongside it. "Lucas ran away! Harland's was robbed!" he hollered. It was all excitement for Ben, a big dumb movie. He was too little to understand. I blinked back tears and stared at the ground as Dad hurried inside the house. I'd just about cleared the yard of grass by the time they called us in.

"We're going to look for Lucas," Mama told us.

"Where?" I asked, ready to join them.

"Up in the hills," Daddy answered. "We'll hike the pony paths and look around a little."

"I think he's close by," Lindy added. "He wouldn't leave me."

Suddenly I knew she was right. Lucas would never leave her—or me, I almost added. He might have been scared, he might have done something awful, but he wouldn't just take off. I knew he'd have a plan.

"I want you kids to stay here, keep an eye out," Mama told us. "Sidda, you get dinner for your brother and sister."

I ran to the front closet, grabbing Jax's leash and three flashlights. Twilight was settling already.

"Where do you think you're going?" Dad asked.

"With you," I answered, whistling for Jax.

"Not this time, Squirt."

"But . . ."

"But nothing," Mama said, securing the leash on Jax, who bounded up to us excitedly. "I want you safe in one place. Can you do that for me?"

I could, of course. I could stay in the house. But what I couldn't do was stay quiet any longer. Lucas was gone, with his bruised arm and maybe worse. If I'd only told them. I felt like all this was somehow my fault.

"But I have to tell you both something," I said. "It's about Lucas, he—"

Lindy interrupted me. "Ready?" she asked, coming up behind us.

I looked at her crumpled expression, her red cheek. Lucas's secret rattled about in my mouth, but I couldn't get my tongue around the words, couldn't work them out.

"It's going to be okay," Mama said firmly. "We'll find him."

I don't know if it was meant for me, for Lindy, or for herself, but we all nodded in the doorway. And then they were gone.

Searching

After sandwiches and cold soup, we plopped ourselves down in the living room. None of us knew what to do, so Sidda took Ben upstairs to read him a story. I headed out to the barn.

Snort nickered when he saw me, and I went to him, pressing my head against his smooth face and inhaling. The sweet smell of hay filled my nose, but it didn't have its usual comforting effect. In the stalls, the patients' cages were quiet, except for the nocturnal opossums, who were wriggling out of their pouch, ready for the night.

"Hey, little guys." I scooped one gently in my hand and moved to the barn door. In the purple twilight, I watched the beams of flashlights bouncing off the pony trail, like little lightning bugs bobbing up the hill. *"Lu-cas!"* the voices called. It felt safe hearing them on the hill.

But then there was another noise. From the direction of the cabin. A slow creaking noise. I peered into the darkness, moving carefully toward it. I heard it again.

"Lucas?" I called softly. "Is that you?"

A shadow shifted on the porch. My heart raced, and I turned to the hill. The flashlights were growing farther away, moving up into the tree line.

"Lucas?" I whispered. I tiptoed across the yard and stopped at the porch. No one was there. But someone had been. The rocking chair was still moving, back and forth, back and forth. My heart pounded in my chest and the little opossum squirmed in my hand.

"Let's go," I said.

I turned back for our barn, feeling all the while like eyes were on me. *Stand up tall,* I told myself. Twice I looked over my shoulder. I was almost in the safety of the barn when someone stepped from the darkness.

"Lucas!" I practically yelled.

"Nope," said a voice. A gravelly voice.

I halted as Carl Dunn stood swaying in front of me, a crooked smile plastered across his face.

"Why aren't you looking for Lucas?" I asked, my voice catching.

"I am." He sneered. "You hiding him in here?"

I shook my head and ducked past him into the barn.

"What you got there?" he asked, pointing to the opossum baby in my arms.

"Nothing," I said, cupping the baby protectively. Carl Dunn's breath was right powerful, filling the doorway. It reminded me of an old bottle we'd found floating in our river one day, an amber liquor washing back and forth inside it as it bobbed along. When Ben had fished it out and unscrewed the cap, we'd recoiled at the smell—a stale vinegar that made our eyes water. The same smell filled the air now. I stood frozen, unable to decide if I should just walk away or run.

"Let me see that," he said, pointing at the opossum.

I shook my head again. "He's sick," I lied, taking a step backward.

Mr. Dunn cocked his head, the crooked smile disappearing. "Give it here. I won't hurt it." He took a swig from a bottle in his hand, and the sour smell washed over me. Images flashed: the bruise on Lucas's arm, the animal patients. Outside, the sky was dark. Why hadn't I turned on the lights?

Carl Dunn reached for the opossum baby cradled in my arms, and I reeled back. I felt my throat swell with a scream so powerful my chest was ready to burst. The kind of scream you dream about in nightmares. But, when I opened my mouth, nothing came out. And then a light opened up the night around us, a white flashlight that lit up the barn doorway, blinding us both.

"Franny?" I ran toward Mama's voice. "Is that you?"

Lucas's father stepped back into the shadow, the bottle behind his back. "Let me guess, no luck," he said and chuckled coldly.

"What are you doing here?" Mama asked, her eyes narrowing.

"She was calling for Lucas. I came to see if he was here."

"He's not," I said, feeling braver with Mama beside me. I hurried to the light switch and flicked it on.

"Franny, I told you to stay in the house." Dad appeared in the newly lit doorway and fixed me with a stern look. He looked just as sternly at Lucas's father, who had started inching his way back toward the cabin. "We'll look again tomorrow, but I'll be listening tonight," he told Carl Dunn.

Dad stayed with me in the barn while I settled the opossum baby back in his bed. We checked the patients together. Birds, turtles, and mice. They were accounted for and quiet. But, still, I felt uneasy leaving them.

"Dad, do you think Lucas is okay?" I asked as we filled their water bowls for the night.

Dad turned on the pump, rinsing the turtle bowl carefully, then carried it back to Speed Bump. "I hope so, Squirt, I really do."

"What's going to happen?" I asked, following him into the stall.

"I don't know," Dad said. He lowered himself onto an old bench by the cages and motioned for me to sit beside him. "Lucas and Lindy are good people, Franny. But they're in a bad situation."

I leaned my head against his arm. "We have to help them," I whispered.

Daddy nodded. "We're trying, honey. It's a strange thing, offering help. Sometimes the people who need it most don't want to take it. Or don't know how to."

It didn't make sense to me. "So what do you do?" I asked.

"You keep trying," Dad said, rubbing my head. "You just keep trying."

That night I sat up in bed for a long time watching the barn through my window, thinking about the patients tucked inside, and about Lucas outside. Nothing was turning out like it was supposed to. Not even in *The Yearling*, a story I wasn't sure I liked anymore. I read for hours, while Sidda snored across the room. I turned page after page, trying so hard to forget my own worries that before I knew it I'd turned the last one. I leaned back against my pillows, hands trembling at what I'd read. Flag and Jody gone, just like Lucas.

I wondered if it was true, what Jody's father told him: that we are all alone in this world. That no matter how much we want things to be good, there is also bad. And that there is no way around it, but to keep on going.

I pictured Jody setting out in his boat, floating away from

his house and his family. Was that what Lucas was doing? I wished I could tuck him away in our barn with all the orphans. It was a long time before I could finally sleep, imagining Lucas curled safely in the hay, snoring soundly while the opossum babies tiptoed through the night beside him.

Free

Mama was right; it was time to let the swallows go. We all needed something good to focus on. August's first week had ended, the sticky heat of July still rolling after us into another summer month. I had hoped for promise at the week's end, for some sign of good to come: a rain cloud, the return of Lucas. But things only seemed to grow worse.

The police had come by again that morning, stopping first at the cabin, then at our house. It was Sunday. Lucas had been gone two nights, and there was still no word. Now, there was a warrant for his arrest.

When Mama sat me down at the kitchen table to talk to Officer Price my heart pounded. I thought of all the things I knew, all the things I felt, but it turned out I didn't know much of anything. I didn't know where he was. I didn't know if he'd taken the money. I hadn't seen him since the afternoon in the driveway. I knew no more than Mama or the Bees or Lindy. Maybe I even knew less. It was a powerful relief, not having to betray his trust. And yet it left me feeling as empty and useless as a dried husk in the field. For the first time I realized that maybe I didn't know Lucas Dunn at all.

So I turned to the animals. In the dark barn I watched the swallows flutter about the hay. They were grown now. That week they'd been swooping and diving after insects, all by themselves. But wouldn't you know it, each night they'd crowd back into their nest, calling for their supper. Mama said they were getting too dependent. She said it was time.

Daddy thought we should hold a proper ceremony, being that they were the first patients to leave the hospital. So I decorated their cage with little paper wings and made an event of it. The whole family came, even Sidda. Grandma Rae showed up, donning her driving hat and clucking at the dust gathering on her good shoes. But I was holding out hope for Lucas.

Dad carried the decorated cage up the path into the hills behind our house, and we followed. It was early in the afternoon. I wanted to give those babies the rest of the day to settle into their new world before night fell.

"This is a good spot," Mama said. We'd stopped by a quiet clearing at the edge of the woods. I looked for signs of life below, but the cabin was quiet, the yard empty.

"Chances are these babies will return, either to our barn or to one of the neighbors'," Dad said, setting the cage in the tall grass. "And if we're lucky they'll come back year after year to raise their own babies."

Ben clapped his hands. And maybe it was selfish of me, but I liked the thought of that. Those babies coming home to me.

"Franny, will you do the honors?" Mama asked. I looked around one more time for Lucas, then opened the tiny door. The five birds peered at me.

"You were good patients," I told them. "Now go make

yourselves a home. And look out for barn cats!" I backed away. The others did, too, moving slowly. And then we waited. But the swallows didn't move.

"Stupid birds," muttered Sidda. "Don't they know they're free?"

Mama nudged her, and we held our breath. It took a long time, but finally a swallow hopped to the door. He perched warily on the edge, blinked, and flew away. The others zoomed out behind him. They zigzagged together, dipped toward the trees, and then disappeared.

"There they go!" yelled Dad.

"Good luck, little guys," Mama called.

Ben started crying and Grandma Rae hugged him. "You liked those dirty little birds, didn't you?" she whispered.

I couldn't talk. I hadn't expected them to be gone so fast.

And with that, everyone headed back down the trail. Ahead of me, the empty cage swung in Dad's hands.

"You did it, Franny," Mama whispered in my ear.

I nodded, my throat too tight to answer, as we walked together. The others hurried on down the trail, Ben and Sidda laughing, Grandma Rae fussing over the dirty hem of her dress. They carried on as if nothing had happened. But I couldn't help it; the sobs just climbed up into my throat and poured out of me. I sat down in the grass, overcome and empty.

Mama kneeled down next to me. "Oh, honey," she said, pulling me into her like a current. "It's a sad old story, the story of us mothers. It's what we do. We love something right full up, till the love just spills over. Now don't you worry; you filled those babies up good. They'll make their way."

"But what if they get lost? Or what if they get hurt and don't let someone help them?" I couldn't help but worry.

"Those babies are fine, Franny," Mama assured me.

But somewhere others were not. It seemed that hurt had surrounded me that summer, had always been there. I just hadn't seen it.

I cried hard. I cried for all the babies in the world, the animals and the humans. For the babies with no mothers or bad fathers. For Lucas, for Lindy, for myself. I cried until there were no tears left. Mama rocked me in the meadow, the colors dancing off the rocks around us. I closed my eyes, but the colors burned behind my lids. The black of the orchard fields, the cool blue bruise of Lucas's arm, the brown flash of wing in the woods. When the tears finally stopped, Mama pushed my hair aside and kissed me on the nose. I caught my breath. I pulled myself up. This time I walked next to her, letting my hands swing, meadow grass tickling my fingertips.

I only looked back once, searching the cloudless sky. It was empty. And then I saw it. Below the sky, a flicker of blue denim in a nearby tree, a bobbing branch that shook the leaves. Two tanned feet tucked themselves quickly back onto the limb of the big oak and my breath caught in my chest. He hadn't missed it after all.

Basket

I started leaving food by the barn. I'd gather things from the kitchen, wrap them in a dish towel, and place them in an old basket. At first Mama pretended she didn't know, but then she began handing me things. A jar of sweet peaches, a loaf of warm bread. "Add these to your basket," she said.

The same afternoon we said goodbye to the swallows, I set the basket by the barn door. All afternoon the basket remained, untouched in the shade. By nightfall, I heard a noise, but it was just a fat raccoon outside my window. I'd about given up when the next morning it was gone.

And that's how it went. The basket would always reappear, the food eaten, a treasure in its place. First, a pinecone. I rolled it between my fingers and inhaled the forest smell, sticky sweet. The second time it was a wild rose, all the prickers removed, the smooth petals tinged with pink. Wordless messages left in a basket. And so I kept each one, hidden in a shoe box under my bed, like love letters.

"Do you know where he is, Franny?" Mama asked me. I didn't, of course. But I knew he was out there. And it was something I just could not tell Mama. Because being a mother, she'd have to inform Lindy. And there was no telling what would happen then. We each had our alliances, and it was the hardest thing to break the one I had with Mama. And so I shook my head and crossed my fingers behind my back. It was the only big lie I'd ever told, and it parked itself like a lump of coal in my stomach.

Lindy kept coming, asking if we'd seen anything.

"He'll come back," Mama assured her. But Lucas's father didn't seem to worry. The cold chink of bottles on the porch floor echoed through each night. I couldn't understand how Lindy let him stay, her own boy gone, her cheek still red. But Mama said not to judge, that all we could do was help if she asked for it. It was hard. Even Mama was getting tired, waiting for her to ask.

I couldn't sleep at night. I'd lie awake until Sidda's soft snores filled the room, before reaching under my bed. Lucas's gifts fell from the shoe box, the moon spilling over them. A round pebble, a grass bracelet, two red leaves. I held these treasures in my hands, pressing each one to my cheek before tucking the box beneath my bed again; worrying if what I was doing was wrong, and wondering what gift the basket would hold tomorrow.

Secrets

"Tell me a secret," Izzy whispered to me, dropping a five-dollar bill in my coffee can.

I jumped. "I don't have any!" I almost shouted, pretending to count the Animal Funds. Did Izzy know about Lucas?

It was the Friday Bee. Lucas had been gone a week and the money from Harland's had not been found or returned. The drought was weighing on everyone's minds, pressing its relentless heat against our skin till our temples throbbed and tempers ran short.

Izzy sat down with a wheezy huff. "Well, I'm bored and it's hot, and a little secret would cheer me up."

"Secrets are for sinners," Grandma stated, her eyes steady on the quilt. A tree trunk wound its way up into the pale blue patchwork sky, where Grandma carefully stitched the wing of a white bird perched in a branch. Dotty and Faye were working on small patches, gray and brown animal-like shapes that I couldn't quite make out. The quilt was nearly done, its patchwork expanse rippling over the ladies' laps like a leafy waterfall.

"Oh, come off the roof, Rae," Izzy said, grabbing a small gray patch. "You got secrets."

"Grandma does?" I asked in disbelief.

"Wouldn't you like to know?" Izzy said, pinching me playfully.

"I got one!" Dotty admitted with a shy grin. We looked at her expectantly. "I sometimes lick the frosting off the cakes I bring to the church coffee hour."

Grandma Rae cringed. "Dotty! That's disgusting."

Dotty sank in her chair.

"That's okay," Mama volunteered, with a wink. "I'll still eat them."

"My secret's better!" Izzy said.

But it was Faye Wakeman who went next. "Well, last week at Harland's, Mavis Plunk came in and complained that I was too slow on the cash register. Said my math skills were about as good as my cornfields. So I picked up her box of denture cream and hollered, 'Price check on false teeth cleaner.' " Faye grinned, showing all her teeth, and we roared with laughter.

"Mine is still better," Izzy said.

But no one was listening.

"What about you, Mama?" Sidda asked.

Mama paused at her easel, the beautiful red jacket of her painted woman fluttering where her brush left it. "Well, let's see," she said.

I looked at Mama carefully. What secrets could she have?

"Once," Mama began, "a long time ago, a gallery owner showed my paintings in Tulsa. Daddy and I got dressed up and went into the city. It was a beautiful night." She stopped, smiling into the distance as if greeting her old self. "That night a gentleman offered to buy one for a lot of money. It was my favorite, a golden hayfield. We really needed that money. I was about to have another baby." Mama winked at me. "But Daddy wouldn't hear of it. He knew I loved it too much."

"So that was it?" Sidda asked.

"No. After the show closed, that same man called me. He asked me to come back to Tulsa and paint a mural in his office building. I'd need to move there for a while, but he offered to cover our expenses. Said it would show my talent off to the world."

"Did you go?" Sidda asked.

Mama smiled sadly. "Of course not. I had you, and Franny on the way. I couldn't leave that." She shook her head, and looked at the paintbrush in her hand. "I never told anyone about the offer that man made to me, not even your dad."

We grew real quiet then, the swift swish of brush on canvas filling the room. When I looked up again, Grandma was staring at Mama in a way I'd never seen before. Almost softly.

"Well, that's a mighty sad story, but I still haven't had my turn," Izzy said and sighed.

"Just tell us then," Grandma scoffed.

"It's a doozy, but it's not just mine." Izzy elbowed Grandma Rae, who elbowed her right back.

"Tell us!" I begged.

Izzy hesitated, eyeing Grandma. "All right for you, Rae. I'm sharing it."

Grandma rolled her eyes.

"What? What is it?" Sidda asked.

We were dying to know.

"The worst!" Izzy said, her eyes dancing mischievously.

"Oh, stop," Grandma Rae scolded her.

"Not in front of the children!" Dotty said, her eyes darting from Izzy to us. Dotty knew, too? Now we were intrigued.

"Please tell!" Sidda begged.

Izzy set her hands on the table and leaned forward dramatically. "One year, about forty years ago, we shared a town garden. We were young girls then, newlyweds without any children yet. We set it up right by the river and took turns watering. I did the beans, Dotty did the tomatoes, and your grandma did the peppers."

"Don't forget the eggplant!" Faye added.

"What's the big deal about a garden?" Sidda frowned.

"I'm getting there," Izzy said with a smile. "Well, that summer was a scorcher, almost as bad as this one. So one day, after lugging the buckets back and forth, I said to myself, 'This is crazy. I'm going in that river before I melt.' But of course I had no bathing suit."

"So what'd you do?" I asked.

"I went in my birthday suit."

"Your what?" Sidda asked.

"I skinny-dipped!" Izzy said.

Dotty looked away, her cheeks glowing red.

"By the town garden? In public?" Sidda gasped. Right then, Izzy took on a new light for both of us.

"You bet your bottom!" Izzy smiled. "Then your grandma came by."

Grandma Rae sat up straighter. "I told her she was crazy. Plumb crazy."

"And?" Izzy prodded.

"And then I joined her." Grandma Rae said it matter-of-factly.

Sidda and I dropped our jaws. It was one of the greatest shocks I had ever experienced. Like pickles and ice cream, skinny-dipping and Grandma Rae did not go together.

"More tea?" Grandma asked, as if Izzy had merely told us about the weather. And then everybody laughed, except Sidda, who kept right on staring at them as if she'd had the wind knocked out of her. But I knew what she was feeling.

It's a strange thing, seeing family in that way. I'd only ever seen Mama as a mother, and Rae as simply a grandma. It never occurred to me that they could have existed before me, could do something as crazy as skinny-dip in the town river. It was a small betrayal. And though we laughed about it then with girlish embarrassment, I understand now what I learned that day. That the world outside our barnyard fence was large and strange, a shock to the gauzy comfort I had wrapped myself in all those years.

The Rain Dance

"What book are you on?" This time I was doing the asking. Pearl was too busy driving me crazy.

All evening, Pearl had paced my room, trying to find an appropriate place to lay out her sleeping bag. We were supposed to be having a sleepover at her house, but Mable had caught a cold. We'd moved the location to my house, something we didn't normally do, since Pearl felt my room had inferior sleeping arrangements. So far the floor was too dangerous ("Heaven knows what's living under your bed!") and the rug was too fluffy ("Allergens! I have a very sensitive nose, you know").

"What about my bed?" I offered. "We can bunk together."

Pearl frowned. "How clean are your sheets?"

That had done it, so I'd asked the meanest thing I could think of, feeling like the horrible person I was as soon as the words tumbled from my mouth. But Pearl was smiling.

"My fifteenth," she practically sang.

"Your what?"

"Technically fifteen, but almost sixteen."

I stared at her. "Wow, you and Nancy really hit it off!"

"Oh, I quit on Nancy. She took too long." Pearl spread her sleeping bag on Sidda's side of the room and stood back, scanning the floor appreciatively.

"So what are you reading?"

Pearl fiddled with one of her red curls. "Just some books with Mable," she answered hesitantly.

"With Mable?" I asked suspiciously.

"Actually, Mable is very advanced for a baby. She likes all kinds of genres."

"A baby who says *woof*?"

Pearl frowned. "She says *meow*, too, you know."

I laughed, picturing the look on Mrs. Jones's face. "So what *advanced* books are you and Mable reading?" I pressed.

Pearl bit her lip and whispered, "*Teddy Bear Goes to the Beach.*"

"Pearl, that's cheating!"

"It is not!" she cried. "They're real books."

"For *babies*!" I retorted.

She slumped on the bed. "You don't know what it's like!" Poor Pearl. Driven to baby books by her mother. Just then a car door slammed outside. I jumped.

"Who's here?" Pearl asked.

Mama and Daddy had taken Ben to an early movie. Sidda was at a friend's. But it was too early for any of them to be home. I went to the window, half expecting to see the police again. Half hoping for word of Lucas. But it was the Busy Bees, pulling into our driveway in Grandma Rae's black town car. They passed the house and parked below, just behind the barn. What could they be doing?

My heart pounded. "I'll be right back," I told Pearl.

Before the Bee had ended that day, I'd gone out to feed the animals. I'd run into Grandma on her way out, the quilt tucked protectively under her arm. It was the first time she'd taken the quilt home since the Bees had started it.

"Is it done? Can I see it?" I'd asked her.

"Not quite," she'd said with a shake of her head. "There's a little something still to do."

And with that she'd headed outside with the others, where the ladies had whispered among themselves in the driveway. There had been a lengthy discussion, with plenty of pointing to the sky, where a full moon was already visible. It was a pale moon, faded into the blue of the late day. I had wondered what it all meant.

Now they were back in my yard, dressed in brightly patterned skirts, staring up at the twilight. I followed their gaze from the window. There, hanging low above our barn, the full-bellied moon glowed strong.

I busied Pearl with making popcorn while I hurried outside. I stepped off the porch into the evening as the Busy Bees tiptoed past our barn. I followed as they made their way to the trail, holding their skirts up out of the grass as they climbed the hill. Quietly I crept behind: heel, toe, heel, toe. The way my fourth-grade teacher described how Native Americans once moved through the woodlands.

Halfway up the hill the Bees paused in a clearing of pines, and I lowered myself behind a boulder. One by one, they kicked their shoes off, standing barefoot in a half circle.

"Join hands," sang Grandma Rae. And then it began. Grandma led, dipping and swaying just a little, and the ladies followed, their skirts swooshing around their bare feet. I remembered what Mama said: *These girls can conjure up the rain.* I pressed myself against the rock, feeling a little like a spy. A gentle breeze stirred around us, and the sky darkened. They moved faster.

The Busy Bees murmured the sacred lines at first, then again, more loudly. The wind picked up, licking at my neck. The circle surged.

Dance in a field to the crickets' tune,
a full-moon sky in the afternoon.

Louder and louder they chanted, hands swinging, heads raised to the heavens. The dust of the summer rose around them like a smoke cloud. Above us the sky shifted, and clouds tumbled. A hard wind began to blow, rustling the grass, bending the young trees.

I sucked in my breath at the strange scene before me. These were not the old ladies who gathered in my dining room with tired feet and soft voices. They became something else, moving like that on the hill: heads thrown back, holding tight to each other, feet pounding a dusty rhythm. Before me was a tribe.

The air grew sharp and cold, and I ducked my head when

something stung my eye. Rain! The ladies spun, a swirling blur of bodies, while the sky rumbled above. It was raining. I turned and ran down the hill, jumping over rocks as the sky opened up above me and the first pelts of rain hit my back.

Our truck was back in the driveway, and Dad, Ben, and Mama were scurrying around in the growing darkness.

"Get the sheets!" Mama hollered, yanking the clothes from the line.

Ben and I rolled the barn doors closed against the slicing rain.

"Run!" I shouted, as we scrambled across the muddy yard.

Inside, we slapped shut windows that had been open all summer and closed doors tightly behind us.

"Where were you?" Pearl demanded as I toweled myself off in the living room.

Ignoring her, I turned to my parents, who were wiping our muddy prints from the doorway. "Did you see them?" I asked Dad, breathless.

"Who?"

"The Bees!"

I pointed toward the barn, but by then the drive was empty, the tire tracks washed clean away.

Fire and Water

Outside the sky flashed, black clouds rolling over our house. When the lights went out, we huddled around the stone fireplace, passing popcorn from lap to lap. Ben fell asleep in Dad's arms, and Mama stretched out on the blanket beside me.

"Tell me," she said.

And so I did.

I told her about the bare feet pounding in the dust and the thumping chants, the swirling skirts and the rolling sky. Sidda's and Pearl's eyes widened suspiciously in the firelight, but it didn't matter. Mama nodded, and I knew she believed. When the fire died down, we went to listen to the rain in our beds.

Hours later, I awoke, thunder and lightning flashing outside my window. I peered outside. There, in the dark sky, our barn glowed. Orange and yellow lines, tracing the barn roof, licking the walls. But it wasn't lightning.

ooo

I don't remember screaming *fire*, though Daddy said I woke up the whole house. I also don't remember who called the police, or who ran outside first. I do remember the feeling in my stomach, the wash of heat and pain and fear that filled me up, and the smell of wet grass burning my nose as I ran into the storm.

"Stand back!" yelled Dad as he yanked at the barn door. Through the smoke I saw Snort's head rearing back, his eyes rolled white. Mama ran in with the fire extinguishers, aiming them at the loft, where the flames grew.

"Get the animals!" I cried.

There was a lot of yelling as we uncoiled the hose and

worked the pump, Jax dashing nervously around us. Daddy trotted Snort through the door to Sidda, who shut him safely in the small pen two paddocks away. Pearl appeared with buckets, passing them to Dad, who threw them at the ladder where the flames were climbing down.

When there was a steady stream of water soaking the walls, I went straight to the stalls, hauling cages out of the smoky darkness.

"Franny, get out," Dad yelled. "You'll get hurt!"

Someone rushed in behind and grabbed me. It was Mama, and she looped one arm around me and scooped up the mice with the other.

"Hurry!" she cried.

We emptied the first stall, dropping the cages on the wet grass outside. Two boxes of mice, and a baby squirrel. Back in the second stall, Mama grabbed Speed Bump. Behind her, the opossums squeaked in the smoke.

"Stay with me!" Mama yelled, hurrying out. But instead, I raced to the opossums and yanked on their door. The latch was stuck. I yanked again, rattling the whole cage, but it wouldn't open. The opossums trembled inside.

"Everyone out," Dad yelled from the doorway. "Now!"

I tried hoisting the cage up onto my shoulder, but it was too heavy. "I'll be back," I told the opossums. I covered my mouth and ran for the door, right into Daddy, who'd come for me.

"Daddy," I screamed. "It's the opossums; their door is stuck, we have to get them!"

He looked at the barn, at the flames racing up and down its sides, and pulled me outside. "No, Franny, it's too dangerous." He coughed.

"We can't leave them," I cried, turning to Mama.

The tears on her cheeks glowed eerily in the orange light. "I'm so sorry, honey. I'm so sorry." Mama pulled me tight, leading me away from the barn, to where Sidda and Pearl sat beside the cages with Jax. "Stay here," she ordered.

Pearl took my hand, and we huddled together, faces flickering as we watched the flames. Jax whined and wiggled nervously beside us.

"It's okay, boy," I said. But I knew it wasn't. I stared carefully at the barn. The left side was only smoking, as the fire roared largely on the right. There was the side door. I still had time.

"Where are you going?" Pearl asked, as I stood.

"It's okay, I'm just checking on Snort." I hurried away, down the side of the hill to where Snort huddled in the far corner of the pen. It was strangely quiet and clear; Snort whinnied nervously. There was no time to comfort him. Once in the safety of the darkness, I turned back, creeping along the fence line, to the barn. As I neared it, I could feel the heat, taste the smoke in the air. There was a sudden crackling noise beside me, a twig breaking on the other side of the fence. I turned, half expecting to see Pearl chasing after me. But there was no one.

Mama and Daddy stood in front of the barn, aiming the hose at the loft. They didn't see me open the side door and hurry back inside.

The smoke was thicker now, swallowing the stalls, rising into my lungs. Coughing, I dropped to the floor and crawled to the rear stall.

"I'm back," I called, rushing to the opossums. They were curled together, pressed against the rear of the cage. I couldn't tell if they were still alive or not. Again, I tried to hoist the large cage onto my shoulder, but it wouldn't budge. I yanked and tugged, dragging it halfway off the hay bale. Above me the barn roared.

"It's too heavy!" I cried out. But no one was there to hear. No one knew where I was. I pulled again, then again, with all my might. I didn't have much time. Finally the cage lurched forward, tumbling on top of me, and we landed together in the dirt. The opossums rolled around inside.

I could hear the flames through the beams in the ceiling. They were speaking in tongues, hissing and spluttering. I tried to wiggle out from under the cage, but I was pinned.

The babies will die, I thought. *All those lullabies and feedings and checkups.* And then it occurred to me: so would I. I closed my eyes and screamed. And then my chest lightened, the cage lifting slowly off of me.

"Franny," a voice shouted.

In the smoky haze, Lucas was reaching for me, pulling me up. He yanked the cage free and we dashed out of the stall, out of the barn as the roof creaked above us, out into the night, where my mother swept me up and my father cried out in shock. Fire trucks lined our drive, great spirals of water streaming toward the barn. But it was too late. We collapsed under the wet spray and watched the roof cave in before us.

Ashes

Lucas and I caught our breath on the grass, unable to take our eyes off the barn. Mama scurried back into the house to check on Ben, who had slept through all of it. Daddy, finally sure that we were safe, slumped against the fence as the firemen worked. Before us the entire barn glowed orange, the spirals of water from the fire hose toppling the timber with its force.

When Sidda appeared with towels to wipe the smoke and soot from our faces, the spell was broken.

"At least we got everyone out," Lucas said, turning to face me. He was soaked, his hair plastered against his forehead, mud streaked across his cheeks. He had never looked more handsome.

"You're back." I coughed, reaching to touch him to be sure.

But Lucas shook his head. "I'm leaving, Franny. I came back for my mom."

"Now?" I looked at the burning barn and the trucks lining our driveway. My mind raced.

"My dad's passed out," he whispered urgently. "We haven't got much time."

"Where will you go?" I asked.

"I don't know yet."

"Stay here. We'll help you."

He shook his head. "No one can help with this."

I felt out of my league. And selfish. Here was Lucas trying

to save his mother, and I was worried about the questions I wanted answered. I glanced over my shoulder at Sidda and Pearl, seated behind us on the wet hill.

"Wait, let me get Mama. She'll know what to do." I was pleading now.

"There is one thing you can do," Lucas said, standing up.

I stood with him.

He nodded in the direction of Lindy's potting shed. "I need your help."

"Anything!" I cried.

"Go to the shed, tomorrow. You'll know what to do."

"What's in it?" I asked.

Lucas shook his head. "Wait until morning," he said. "I trust you."

"That's it?"

"That's it," he said.

I looked at his drenched shirt, his dirty face. And I knew what I had to do.

"Wait here," I told him. "I have to give you something."

I raced up to the house, stopping only at my bedroom dresser. I took what I needed from the top drawer before hurrying back outside again. Lucas was at the edge of the yard, already moving toward the cabin. Already moving away.

"Take this," I said, handing him my coffee can.

He frowned. "I can't take your Animal Funds, Franny."

But I pushed it toward him again, and he did not refuse.

"I won't be able to call you, Franny, or write. Not for a while."

I nodded, tears stinging my eyes.

"I will, though. Someday I will, I promise."

I wanted to tell him to be careful, to come back, to promise. But I just nodded like a little girl, tears spilling stupidly down my cheeks.

Lucas took my hand, turning the palm up in his sooty fingers.

I shivered.

"Remember," he whispered, tracing my palm. And then he leaned in, his lips brushing mine gently at first, then firmly, all the promises and pain of the summer passing between us.

When I finally opened my eyes, he was walking into the darkness.

Taxi

As we sat stunned on the wet hillside, Grandma Rae's fancy black car rolled in behind the trucks.

"Thank the Lord, thank the Lord," she wheezed, hurrying from one of us to the next in her robe and bedroom slippers and smothering us in her embrace, even Pearl. Soda-can-size curlers peeked out from under her floral scarf, crushing my cheek as she hugged me once more for good measure. "I heard the sirens and saw the trucks head out this way. When no one answered the phone . . ." She dabbed her eyes and looked away. Then she turned her attention to the rows of cages, the patients huddling inside. Grandma Rae shook her head sadly and pointed to her car. "Load 'em up!" she ordered.

"What?"

"Quick, child, before I change my mind." Grandma Rae opened the trunk of her town car.

Surely she didn't mean what I thought she did. "But you hate them," I reminded her. "They're dirty, germy, rotten, smelly animals. *Wild* animals."

Grandma tilted her head, considering this, and nodded. "Yes, yes, all of that is true. But they are *in need*. You can keep them in my shed. Not quite as big as your barn, but there's plenty of shade. Now, come on." She motioned to the trunk again.

"But they'll suffocate in there," I protested.

"Oh, dear, I guess we don't want that." She sighed and mopped her brow with a monogrammed hankie. Clearly this was more than Grandma Rae had bargained for, certainly more than *those in need* required of a person. Even a Christian. "All right, the backseat it is. Just don't scratch the leather." Grandma Rae opened the door dramatically and covered her nose.

"Why, Rae!" Mama exclaimed, her face brightening. "I can't believe it."

Grandma cringed as I lowered Speed Bump onto the car seat.

"*The Lord* will be real proud," Mama said, squeezing her arm.

"It's only temporary," Grandma warned.

When the backseat was fully loaded, Grandma Rae got behind the wheel. She adjusted her rearview mirror so she wouldn't see the patients. "Lord have mercy. Never thought I'd have rats for passengers," she muttered.

Ben and I stood outside the car, waving goodbye. He squealed in delight. "Guess what you are, Grandma?" he asked.

"Crazy?"

"No. The Animal Taxi!"

Grandma, pretending not to hear this, blared the horn at the firemen and roared out of the driveway. "Make way, men, I've got rats in transport!" she called.

The Bottle

Looking at the smoky remains the next morning left a powerful hole in my heart. When the day broke over the pile of rubble that used to be our barn, the Fire Department began their search. Detective Roy and several others scoured the site. This is what they found: a singed English saddle with the brass nameplate "Shadow," the wire cage that Mama saved Speed Bump from, and an empty whiskey bottle.

"Know anyone who could've been up in your loft?" Detective Roy asked Dad.

"It wasn't a hay fire, from the heat?"

"No, sir, this time Mother Nature's innocent," Detective Roy informed us.

Dad took the bottle, and I followed his gaze as it fell on the cabin. For the first time I noticed the blue truck still parked in the driveway. How could that be?

"They're still here," I hollered, forgetting the barn, the bottle in Dad's hand.

"Who?" Detective Roy stepped forward.

"Lucas and Lindy," I said, turning to Mama. "They were supposed to run away last night. Something's wrong!"

"Something is wrong," Mama said quietly, her brow wrinkling worriedly. She motioned to the barn, the trucks. "All of this going on, and they never came out last night."

Detective Roy interrupted. "Let me get this straight. Your missing neighbor reappears last night, your barn goes up in flames, and he told you he was running away with his mother?" He addressed my father. "Any reason to suspect a member of the Dunn family?"

Daddy looked at me, and then back at Detective Roy. "Perhaps you should talk to them, yes," he said quietly.

It was too much. Detective Roy pulled out a walkie-talkie, his words cutting the smoky air: *arson, missing suspect, grocery store theft.*

I pleaded with Mama. "Lucas needs our help. I meant to tell you everything, honest I did. But I promised Lucas. His arm was all bruised, and then Lindy's face . . ." I turned to the detective. "Lucas didn't burn our barn."

Daddy put his hand on my shoulder. "Franny, no one's saying he did. But there's a lot more going on than you know . . ."

I did know. "Lucas isn't a thief, Daddy. He wouldn't just steal from Harland's. Not for himself."

He sighed. "Franny, sometimes people do desperate things."

Rescue

We watched as police officers circled the cabin, knocking on the front door, peering through the windows.

"Where did you last see him?" Detective Roy asked.

I pointed to the hill. "There. Just after the fire."

He pulled Daddy aside. "You should take your family inside while we search the area."

"But he's innocent!" I cried.

Daddy took my hand. "In the house, Franny. Now."

But I couldn't go. The secrets and the promises rattled around my head, and I just couldn't keep them any longer. I had to tell.

"Daddy, please," I begged.

But before I could speak, the cabin door flew open. Lucas's father teetered in the doorway, fury plastered across his face. Even the detective jumped in surprise.

"Get off my property!" Mr. Dunn yelled.

Instantly, police surrounded the cabin, some drawing their guns. Daddy snatched me up and hurried to the porch.

"What's happening?" I cried. But no one answered me.

"Let's have some tea," Mama said, moving us to the table, away from the scene outside.

"Are Lucas and Lindy okay?" I asked Daddy.

"I don't know, Franny. We have to hope so."

Ben started to cry.

We could hear the police next door, shouting orders to one another, demanding that Lucas's father come out.

My ears strained. Daddy covered my hand in his.

"It'll be okay," Mama whispered as she put the kettle on. "It'll be okay." We all sat at the kitchen table. Pearl and Sidda, Ben and Mama and Daddy and me. We sat for what seemed like forever, staring at each other, afraid to move or speak.

Suddenly there were shouts from the yard. Frantic shouts, followed by the banging of doors and more voices. And then a long, terrible silence. My stomach churned.

Ben whimpered, and Jax got up to lick his face.

Finally, an officer came to our front door.

"We've secured the property," he told us. "It's all clear."

Mama leaped up. "The mother and son?"

"They're fine," he said. "We're taking them in."

And just like that it was over. Mama buried her face in Ben's hair, and her body heaved a long time before the sobs came out. Daddy wrapped his arms around them both, and Pearl ran for the phone to call her mother.

I had to see for myself. I ran to the porch and was halfway down the steps before Daddy caught up with me. He grabbed me by the arm as two police cars roared out of the driveway.

"Lucas didn't do it!" I yelled, struggling to pull away.

But Daddy didn't let go until we were back on the porch and the driveway was empty. Only then did he lean down and look me square in the eyes.

"Franny, he'll be all right."

"Where are they taking them?"

He looked down the road. "To the station. They're going to ask them questions. Find out what happened. It's all over now."

But Daddy was wrong. It wasn't over. There was one promise left that I could keep.

Lost and Found

As soon as the police and fire cars had pulled away, Pearl went home and we stumbled into our beds. When the house was finally still, I snuck outside and across the smoky yard.

The door creaked as I stepped inside the potting shed. Nothing looked different. Lindy's kiln squatted in the dark corner like a potbellied old man. Her vases and bowls lined the shelves, and the workbench was covered in shipping boxes. I scanned the shed floor. What had Lucas meant? I wondered. It was when I turned to leave that I noticed it. It was sitting behind the door. A small zippered sack, the name "Harland's Market" printed on its side. *Oh, Lucas,* I thought.

I wheeled my bike out from under the porch and pedaled quickly down the driveway, the sack in my basket. Despite all that had happened, it was only eight in the morning. The town center was empty, eerily quiet. Turning onto Main Street, I passed the library, the feed store, and town hall, their windows dark and their shades pulled down like sleepy eyelids. Shafts of sunlight spilled over rooftops and crept across shadowed buildings, casting a golden glow. At the north end of the green, Grandma Rae's church steeple sparkled like a beacon, guiding me down the street. I pedaled along the green, its grass dew-glistened as morning mist rose lazily into the air. Something was different. The August-baked air was dappled now, cool and moist with storm droplets. The rain had washed away the dust, the specks of dried earth, and the caked soil, leaving everything rich and moist and slick in its wake. Now, a fertile smell met my nose: the scent of earth, the scent of life.

Harland's was still closed, but the lights were on in back as I pedaled up. Amid the rain-washed scent in the air was something else, something homemade. Baked bread. The smell of it filled the air, making my mouth water something fierce. I'd have to sneak by the early-morning bakers.

I parked my bike against the building, behind a green Dumpster, and pulled the sack from the basket. This was my chance.

There were two bakers in the kitchen, the younger one whistling loudly as she worked. They kept their aproned backs to me as they loaded a nearby cart with steaming loaves of bread.

I edged the door open with my toe. Inch by inch I crept inside, slipping behind a stack of plastic crates.

"Roll these out," the gray-haired baker barked. "And make it fast."

Her younger partner sighed and pushed the wheeled rack out of the kitchen into the store.

Which way was the office? I wondered. I tiptoed from

behind the crates and slunk past the baker. Silently I made my way across the back of the store, searching. Having no luck locating the office, I was heading back in the direction of the bakery when I dropped the sack in the middle of an aisle.

Suddenly there was the squeak of wheels. The bread cart rounded the corner. The younger baker was back. There was no time to get the sack.

I jumped into the nearest aisle, pressing myself against a display of spaghetti sauce jars. The cart wobbled by, a pair of worn-out sneakers stomping behind it. The sack was right in its path.

"Bread's out," the young baker called. She stopped there and wiped her brow. The sack was now directly in front of her cart. Had she not seen it?

"Well, hurry up," called the other baker from the back. "You're slower than a wet week."

The young baker sighed and shook her head. "Slave driver," she muttered.

I stared at the white sack. If only I could reach out far enough . . .

The cart wheels squeaked to life as she turned toward the bakery.

I held my breath.

She ran right over the sack. Bump, bump, went the wheels. But the baker kept on pushing, never once looking down. With the noise and the rattling cart as a shield, I reached out behind her, grabbed the sack, and scooted around the corner.

The door in the corner was closed, the word "Office"

engraved on a plastic gold sign. I breathed a sigh of relief and tried the handle. Locked.

What now? From the front of the store voices erupted, along with footsteps. The morning workers were arriving. I clutched the sack. I had to find the right spot. Not just anywhere. Somewhere obvious, somewhere safe. The footsteps pounded down the aisle, the voices growing closer. I ran for the back door.

Hope

Later that morning, Mama packed us all off to Grandma Rae's, "to check on the animals," she said, but I suspect it was just as much to get away. No one had noticed my disappearance earlier, as I'd returned to find all the members of the family seated with their shock in their own parts of the house.

When Mama rounded us up, Sidda and Ben and I crowded into the car with Jax. It was Ben who glanced back as we pulled away. One look at his face, and I knew what he was seeing. I didn't turn around.

Grandma Rae and the Bees must've known we were coming. No sooner had we pulled up to the front door than Izzy came flying off the porch, plucking each one of us from the car as if she hadn't seen us in years.

"Food's on," she announced, setting her straw hat playfully on Ben's head. She'd kept it simple, one white rose solemnly in the center.

Inside, the table was set, a heaping platter of eggs and bacon and hotcakes.

"Brunch," Grandma explained. "To start the day over."

Faye and Dotty and Grandma scurried about, spoons and saucers flying from all directions. None of us were hungry, but we couldn't stand the thought of any more pained expressions or hurt feelings, so we passed the plates and picked up our forks.

Afterward we sort of spread out. Ben took a comic book out to the porch and Sidda sprawled on the rug in front of the television with Daddy. Mama lowered herself onto the couch and seemed to take a nap behind Grandma's embroidered pillow. While Grandma Rae and the Bees cleaned up, I found myself wandering around, unsure what to do. My body ached with a tiredness so fierce I thought I would collapse. But my arms and legs just wouldn't hear of it. They jittered as thoughts of Lucas and his mother scampered in and out of my head.

Grandma Rae found me at the window. "Have a little rest," she said, draping a blanket on my shoulders. "You can lie down with this."

The colorful quilt spilled onto the floor, familiar squares of green and blue. The Bees' quilt. A lone tree burst into the pale blue sky, its branches reaching for the clouds. And in those branches bobbed animals, animals I recognized. A turtle with a crooked yellow stripe, a whiskered mouse, three opossum babies. Suspended dreamily in a giant tree, my own tree of life.

"When did you . . . ?"

"We have our ways," Grandma Rae said, heading back to the kitchen.

And so I stood, branches wrapped around me, in the hallway of Grandma's parlor, staring at the framed ancestors in the black-and-white photos. My people.

"A rough-looking bunch, aren't they?" Izzy said, coming to stand behind me.

I nodded. "They look like I feel."

"Worse. Those were some tough times, living on the farm in those days."

I didn't say anything. I looked at the drawn faces, the unblinking eyes. Even the family sheepdog stared purposefully from behind two barefoot boys.

"You think you've got it bad now?" Izzy shook her head. "They saw it all. The Dust Bowl of 1936 just about ruined them."

"Ruined?" I asked. I'd heard about the dust bowls, as had every kid growing up in Oklahoma. It was as much a part of our blood as it was the country's history.

"Nineteen thirty-six ruined most," Izzy replied. "Dust storms tore right over the panhandle, ruining the crops and covering houses and farms with dirt. Yes sir, that year was the worst. It left the farmers with no crops to sell and left the country with no wheat. People were poor, Franny. Families had no money, no food. Bellies were so empty mothers cooked root soup month after month."

"Root soup?" I'd never heard of it, but it sounded bad.

"Sure, potato and turnip, whatever you found in the root

cellar. I remember it. My poor mama gave us kids the vegetables, and she sipped the broth."

I stared at Izzy. This wasn't the way Grandma Rae told it. Grandma had always spoken of the hard work, the strong will. I'd known farm life was tough; just the ribby horses strapped to heavy plows told that story. But Grandma had never mentioned the empty bellies.

"What happened?" I asked her.

"Well, this part of the country knew hard times. We'd weathered droughts before, but not like that. You can't imagine it. There was economic depression, sickness, and starvation. Farmers folded, took what little belongings they had, and headed west for places like California."

Izzy paused, her eyes traveling over the faces on the wall. "A lot of families gave up and moved. But not my family. And not the Parkers."

"How'd they get by?" I asked.

"With new farming methods. And the first tractor in the county. Your great-grandfather saw to it."

"He did?" I looked at the overalled man in front of the barn.

"Yep. Hadn't seen anything like it around here before. People thought he was crazy. Of course, with many of the farmers selling off or being forced out, it was an uncertain time. But he was a fighter and he had a vision, and that tractor was his ticket. Came all the way from Iowa, a steel-wheeled crank-start contraption that was god-awful to drive, but it mowed those wheat fields. Harvested twice the fields in half the time. Why, the neighbors were in awe. Soon they were putting up their best horses and cows as down payments on tractors of their own."

I could see it, the waving wheat under a yellow sun, my great-grandfather stationed at the seat of the tractor. Row after row falling away beneath him.

"Some people say it was the tractor that saved our county farms, some people say it was the man who brought the tractor. I say it was hope. These people on the wall, your people, they had hope in their bleakest hour. And that hope runs in a family."

"It does?"

"Sure. Can't you feel it coursing through your veins right now? You're a Parker, Franny. Parkers don't quit." Izzy slapped my behind with a dish towel and returned to the kitchen.

Outside, I hurried past Ben to the shed behind the house where the animals were. I swung open the door, revealing the cages Grandma had carefully stacked. She'd even filled the bowls with fresh water.

Speed Bump ducked her head in her shell. I bent down real close and looked in the turtle's eyes. I pictured my great-grandfather in the dust-filled fields, bumping grimly along on his steel-wheeled tractor, while others packed their bags and shook their heads.

"It's gonna be okay," I told the animals, trying to sound like a Parker.

Aftermath

Lindy was the first to exit the police car when they rolled into the driveway that evening. She stepped out of the passenger side and glanced tiredly at the cabin. Ben and I held our breath at the window. We watched the hefty officer lumber around to the back. When he opened the door, Lucas stepped out.

There would be no charges. At least for Lucas and Lindy. The whiskey bottle from the barn fire was enough to cause the detective to hold Mr. Dunn. They'd found hay from our barn's loft on his clothes. And the scorched toe of his left boot was further proof of his presence at the scene. So he made a half-drunken confession, saying he fell asleep while having a smoke, which he tried to take back when he sobered. But it didn't matter. Later, fingerprints on the bottle would match his. And arson was just the beginning. Lindy would eventually come forward with the rest.

As for the search warrant, it wasn't necessary. The police asked Lucas about the missing money, but it turned out the money wasn't missing after all. The truth was Lucas had no idea how three thousand dollars ended up in the banana case, right in the front window of Harland's Market. Mr. Harland had arrived at work as usual, stopping to read the strange new sign: "Bananas on Sale." And just below, the crisp bills, all three thousand dollars, were neatly stacked among the fruit. It was a mystery, one that would cause a lot of talk around town, and a few raised eyebrows in the Parker house, but a mystery nonetheless.

For those last weeks of summer we pretended things were back to normal. And though it didn't feel quite the same, I was sure it would soon. And so I waited. I waited as summer prepared its surrender, as the green gush of late August gave way to the first yellow promise of fall. I waited as Pearl won second prize for the Aubree Library reading contest, even though she'd done it with a little help from Mable's picture books. I would've thought her mother would have been real put out, being that it wasn't the gold trophy. But she placed the silver one smack-dab in their front window, sparkling for all to see, and Pearl promptly arrived on my doorstep with the second-place check for fifty dollars.

"For your Animal Funds," she said.

"But it's yours," I told her. "You earned it."

Pearl shrugged, looking a bit embarrassed. "We all need help," she said.

And soon things did feel normal again. Almost. On the day Lindy finally threw open the doors of her potting shed once more, I was sure my waiting was over. But it wasn't what I'd wanted. Lindy began to pack.

We gathered in the potting shed while Lindy told us the news. The secret she'd been keeping.

"It's your chance," Mama told her, smiling through her tears as she picked up a jade-green pot. We were seated on the floor staring at the cardboard boxes surrounding us. Sidda,

Mama, Lindy, and me. One by one we gently tucked the pots into beds of tissue and foam for their long journey to California. To a gallery where they would be displayed, not far from the university where Lindy would work in the art department as a teaching assistant.

Everything she deserved, Mama said.

And yet I could not bring myself to feel happy.

"This is my favorite," Mama said, passing Lindy the jade pot. "It reminds me of the fields."

Lindy nodded, turning the pot over and over in her hands. The green of summers past flashed before our eyes. "You hold on to it," she told Mama, handing the pot back. Lindy insisted Sidda and I each choose a piece to keep, to remember her by.

Sidda chose a yellow vase.

"As blond as you," Lindy said. "Did you choose one, Franny?" she asked.

I shrugged. A small vase, watery blue like Lucas's eyes. Lindy kissed me on the forehead.

"Classes start in a few days," she told us. "We have to leave right away."

My stomach fell. My own school started in a few days. The school whose doors would never open to Lucas Dunn. The sadness swelled from my stomach to my throat, and I swallowed hard. After all the bad that had happened, was this a happy ending? I couldn't listen anymore. I stood to leave.

"It's your chance," Mama told Lindy again. But she was looking at me.

I thought of Mama's paintings, stored quietly in our attic.

About her own chance in Tulsa, so long ago. I sat back down with the others

We worked in silence, taping the boxes closed, labeling each in black marker. When we were done we stood, staring at the empty shelves, the clay marks on the floor. Lindy started to cry. "It's the strangest thing," she said. "Lucas and I, we've moved around a lot these last few years. But for the first time, I feel like we're leaving home."

Mama took her hand. "You are," she said.

And so, one late August afternoon, I stood with a pitcher of lemonade, just as I had a couple months before, watching this time as things were loaded onto the truck. First the duffel bags of clothes. Then the potting wheel, followed by the kiln, which Daddy helped to lift. Finally the boxes of books, eight in all, stacked neatly between the coolers of cookies and pies and bread the Busy Bees had insisted Lindy take. But still we couldn't say goodbye. So we dragged it out until dusk, after one last meal of Daddy's famous fried chicken, one last batch of corn on the cob together.

Soon fall would find us, and it would mark more than just a change of season. For us there were new school clothes to shop for and new teachers to meet. For Lucas and Lindy, a final night's sleep in the cabin and a long leafy highway to navigate. After dinner Lucas found me on the back porch tending to the opossums. Grandma Rae's shed was empty. Speed Bump had long since been released into the river behind our house. We hadn't seen her in a while, but Ben never stopped looking. Runty and the other mice had found the upper fields, the squirrels the old maples in the meadow. Only the opossum babies remained.

"You can't hang on to them forever," Lucas whispered from behind. Darkness was just beginning to settle around us, the sky a deep purple-gray.

I nodded, without turning around. "They're nocturnal, you know," I said, looking up at him.

"A twilight release," he mused. "I think I've got time."

And that was it. We gathered them into a cardboard box and headed up the hill, into the woods, behind the black dust of our old barn.

"Here?" Lucas asked, setting the box in the field.

"No, it's got to be perfect," I said.

He sighed patiently and we hiked on, stopping finally at a big birch, right on the fringe of the forest. Below us, the barnyard stretched out in the pale moonlight, the lights of our house glowing warmly, the blue truck packed in the driveway. We stood watching the figures of our families below, their voices trailing up the hill.

I looked at Lucas.

"Ready?" he asked.

I nodded.

We opened the box together, and the opossums stumbled out, sniffing the crisp air suspiciously. I reached out and touched each coarse coat one last time. It took them a few minutes, but they decided the spot was okay after all and ambled into the woods, a little opossum parade.

"Quick," Lucas said. "Make a wish for them."

"For what?"

"How about plentiful seasons?"

My eyes filled, and I wiped them silently, grateful for the darkness so Lucas wouldn't see. But he must've known, for he grabbed my hand and squeezed it hard, holding on tight all the way home.

At the truck the next morning, we all hugged goodbye, and it was a big mess of arms reaching and squeezing, Lindy's and Mama's, Ben's and Sidda's and Daddy's, and lastly mine and Lucas's.

When I held out the worn copy of *The Yearling*, Lucas smiled. "Keep it," he said, pressing the book in my hand.

"You're just like him."

"Who?" he said and laughed. "Jody or Flag?"

I thought about that. The orphan fawn, a thing so beautiful that never really belonged, or the grown boy, making his way into a world harder and brighter than before. "Both," I decided. And then we hugged so tight and held on so hard I thought my chest would burst.

After they drove away, Mama wiped her eyes and Daddy raced Ben back into the house. Sidda gave me a little pat before following them. I was the last one in the driveway, waving the longest, wishing the hardest.

Out of the Dust

Grandma Rae still thanks the Lord no one was injured that hot summer night. At least not the kind of injury a person can see on the surface. As for that, Mama said we'd feel it inside us for a while. The summer that changed everything. I tried to remember what it was like, how the summer fever had crept up on us like a cat, brushing its tail coyly at our legs, rubbing against the backs of our knees, and then sinking its claws in good.

The first thing I learned that year was that good intentions can only get you so far. *Those in need* were not just around us, they were in our very own backyard. And wanting to help just wasn't enough. You could stand all day holding help out, trying to push it in the palm of someone's hand. But that hand had to want it. I like to think my intentions were good. Promising to keep a secret, trying to undo a mistake. Summer may not have turned out like we'd thought, but with the bad surprises there were the good. Like my swallows, who returned to our new barn in the spring. And like Grandma Rae and the Animal Taxi. No turtle has sat on the backseat of her town car since, but she'd do it again, I know.

Another thing I learned is that family comes in all shapes and sizes. And family's not just the people you share your blood with. Take the power of friendship. There are lifelong friends you can't seem to shake, and new friends who find themselves in your backyard. Just like family, a good friend will stand by you, pull you into a living room of laughter, or out of the flames that lick the sky above you. And like with family, there are secrets. I've learned that some secrets a person shouldn't be asked to keep. But there are others that are easy to keep, that are downright delicious. Like the swirling circle of old friends in a wooded grove, the dance that calls the rain. Friendship is a powerful thing.

Finally there is the fever. It's not just the summer fever, I realize that now. It's the fever of love. Love of a small town, an orphaned animal, a boy across the yard. Love has led me to many places, both to and from my family. Like the river that runs through our backyard, the love of my family courses through my veins. It surrounds me. Like the portrait of a young woman in a red coat that hangs over our fireplace. A woman made of flesh and bone by my mother's hand, as fierce and lovely as Mama herself, a portrait of Grandma Rae. I look at my people, the Parkers, on the parlor wall of Grandma Rae's differently now. They are not distant faces separated from me by time. I know them like I know my right hand. And on bad days I remind myself to be hopeful.

As Mama said, some packages arrive on your porch banged up and unrecognizable. You just have to remember what they started out as. Like the postcard I got a week after Lucas left, the edges crushed but the printing crisp and straight. "Thank you, Francesca," it said. "Love, the opossums."

In the end, Lucas was right about plentiful seasons. Although that summer was one of the hardest, it was really the beginning. In me it added to the rings of my tree, the hope and the sadness, the trying and the giving up, and trying all over again. It filled me up, spilling into my branches, unfurling my leaves. My limbs tingled with the energy of it. And I grew.

Acknowledgments

I would like to first thank my agent, Barbara Markowitz, for changing my life one spring day with a scrawled note in my mailbox that said simply, "I like this. A LOT!"

I could not have accomplished this without my editor, Janine O'Malley, at Farrar, Straus and Giroux, whose careful eye and deftly placed Post-it notes guided me across the deep channel of editing, delivering Franny safely to the other side. I am ever grateful for her patience, kindness, and trust.

To everyone at FSG, I thank you for your warm welcome and support. It was more than any new author could have hoped for.

To Ron Olson, English teacher extraordinaire, who first introduced me to Shakespeare and the Romantic poets, as well as the idea that I can and should do this.

From the very beginning, I have been thankful for my family. For my father, my earliest and most avid audience, the original writer in the family. And for my husband, Jason, my first reader, who is not afraid to tell me what I need to hear, and whose keen understanding of the human spirit brings out the best in my characters and helps shape who I most want them to become. I love you all.

Acknowledgments